"James Morrow's novel about early American witchcraft pulls off so many dazzling feats of literary magic that in a different century he'd have been burned at the stake."

Washington Post

"This impeccably researched, highly ambitious novel — nine years in the writing — is a triumph of historical fiction."

Booklist

FOR *The Cat's Pajamas*

"His latest collection demonstrates that his rapier wit has lost none of its edge as it encompasses twisted scenarios ranging from Martians invading Central Park to having the fates of other worlds rest upon the scores of American football games.... All the stories manifest Morrow's penchant for exploring the dark underbelly of technological promise and extracting quirky moral conundrums. Morrow's fans will revel, and first-time readers may find his grim humor making fans of them, too."

Booklist

"Far more entertaining than most of that tedious stuff you've been forcing yourself to read."

Fantastic Reviews

BOOKS BY JAMES MORROW

NOVELS

The Wine of Violence (1981)

The Continent of Lies (1984)

This Is the Way the World Ends (1985)

Only Begotten Daughter (1990)

City of Truth (1990)

The Last Witchfinder (2006)

The Philosopher's Apprentice (2008)

THE GODHEAD TRILOGY

Towing Jehovah (1994)

Blameless in Abaddon (1996)

The Eternal Footman (1999)

SHORT STORY COLLECTIONS

Swatting at the Cosmos (1990)

Bible Stories for Adults (1995)

The Cat's Pajamas (2004)

SHAMBLING TOWARDS HIROSHIMA

JAMES MORROW

Shambling Towards Hiroshima

TACHYON PUBLICATIONS | SAN FRANCISCO

a1

Tachyon Publications

1459 18th Street #139

San Francisco, CA 94107

(415) 285-5615

www.tachyonpublications.com

Series Editor: Jacob Weisman

ISBN 13: 978-1-892391-84-1

ISBN 10: 1-892391-84-8

Printed in the United States of America by Worzalla

First Edition: 2009

9 8 7 6 5 4 3 2 1

ACKNOWLEDGEMENTS

I AM INDEBTED to various friends, relatives, colleagues, and Hollywood historians who consented to shamble through the manuscript of this novella, annotating errors and suggesting improvements, for no reward beyond seeing their names in print. This generous community includes Joe Adamson, Shira Daemon, Justin Fielding, Peter G. Hayes, Laurie Smith Kaczanowska, Joseph Kaufman, Reggie Lutz, Mac McMahon, Christopher Morrow, Glenn Morrow, Fred Ramsey, John Semper, Alain Silver, James D. Smith, Bill Spangler, Marc Wanamaker, and most especially my exquisite wife, Kathryn Morrow. My gratitude also goes to my wonderful agent, Wendy Weil, as well as to the authors of the nonfiction works that inform Syms Thorley's adventures, notably *Hiroshima in America* by Robert Jay Lifton and Greg Mitchell, *Racing the Enemy* by Tsuyoshi Hasegawa, *Monsters Are Attacking Tokyo!* by Stuart Galbraith IV, *Godzilla on My Mind* by William Tsutsui, and *Against Interpretation* by Susan Sontag. And, finally, a snappy salute to Ron Adams and his ectoplasmic emporium, Creepy Classics, for supplying me with so many essential DVDs.

"This thing of darkness I acknowledge mine."
—*The Tempest* v, i

to
Vincent Singleton
my Tennessee Taoist

SHAMBLING TOWARDS HIROSHIMA

I

WHETHER THIS MEMOIR will turn out to be the world's longest suicide note, or instead the means by which I might elude the abyss, only time can tell: a precise interval of time, in fact, the twenty-five hours that stretch between the present moment, Sunday, October 28, 1984, 11:06 A.M., and my presumed departure tomorrow on the noon shuttle to the airport. Right now the other route by which I may exit this sterile Baltimore hotel — the balcony — is the more alluring. I need merely cross the room, slide back the glass door, step onto the terrace, and avail myself of the hundred-foot drop to the parking lot.

Appearances are deceiving. Just because you're reading my story, that doesn't mean I lost my nerve and took the shuttle bus. The proper inference may simply be that I slipped the manuscript into an envelope festooned with stamps and addressed to the Rachel Bishop Literary Agency in New York, then left the package outside my door along with a note asking the hotel management to pop it in the nearest mailbox. Are you reading this, Rachel? I love you, sweetheart. You're the greatest agent a has-been ever had. Assuming you find somebody who can decipher my handwriting, feel free to transcribe these pages, give them a title — *The Day of the Lizard*, perhaps, or *Peasants with Torches*, or *Shambling Towards Hiroshima* — and sell the thing to Doubleday for a big, fat advance, collecting your well-earned ten percent. The balance should go to Darlene. Yes, Rachel, I believe you've finally gotten a bestseller out of me, and it arrives bearing the ultimate seal of authenticity, the author's notorious leap into oblivion, at once swan dive and swan song. True, the NSA may attempt to block publication, but when they go to make their case, the judge will laugh them out of court, especially when he hears about the giant fire-breathing bipedal iguanas.

To tell you the truth, Rachel, I've been dropping hints about the Knickerbocker Project behemoths for over four years now, mostly to my devotees — that is, to admirers of Kha-Ton-Ra the living mummy, Corpuscula the alchemical creature, and Gorgantis, King of the Lizards. The kids aren't interested. Instead they want to know how many yards of rotting gauze I wore in *Curse of Kha-Ton-Ra*. (One hundred fifty, as a matter of fact.) Did I play both roles in *Corpuscula Meets the Doppelgänger*? (Of course I did, O ye of little fanaticism.) Did I really write the script for *Gorgantis the Invincible* under the pseudonym Akira Fukiji? (Not only that, I wrote *Gorgantis Unchained* as Kihachi Ifukabe and *Gorgantis vs. Octopocalypse* as Minoru Natsuke.) By now the fans realize that, sooner or later, I'll manage to bring up my obsession with Überweapons — biological, atomic, and otherwise. They tolerate this tic of mine, but barely. History holds no fascination for them. The politics of atrocity bores them silly.

A Martian would be within his rights to ask why I'm in such low spirits this morning. After all, last night the Wonderama Fantasy Film Convention presented me with a major award, the

Raydo, a name meant to evoke not only the rhedosaurus, that ersatz dinosaur featured in *The Beast from 20,000 Fathoms*, but also the two Rays without whom the movie wouldn't exist — Bradbury, author of the original story, and Harryhausen, stop-motion animator extraordinaire. Were my hypothetical Martian to drop by Room 2014 right now, I would explain that on our planet winning a pewter trophy doesn't feel nearly as good as bottomless despair feels bad.

In my view it's boorish to complain about banquet food, so let me go on record as saying that the chicken croquettes and bean salad at the Wonderama Awards dinner were scrumptious. Predictably enough, everybody squirmed during my acceptance speech — as usual, I railed against the thermonuclear arsenals into whose maw our civilization may soon disappear — and the applause was understandably tepid. Feeling at once piqued and chagrined, I slipped away before the next event, a raffle for a credible facsimile of my Gorgantis suit, which the Wonderama staff evidently got for a steal after the National Science Fiction Museum in Denver went bust.

My Raydo statuette is a rather handsome artifact, featuring not only a skillful reproduction of the rhedosaurus in all his dorsal-plated glory, but also the Maine lighthouse he destroys halfway through the picture. The inscription is eloquent and contains only one error. *Syms K. Thorley, Lifetime Achievement Award, Baltimore Imagi-Movies Society, 1984.* My made-up middle initial is *J*. Where did they get that *K*? I hope they weren't thinking of my eternal nemesis, the egregious Siegfried K. Dagover. That would be the unkindest typo of all.

Today my Raydo will function as a paperweight, securing
each successive page after I've torn it, littered with my scrib-
blings, from the legal pad. I'm equipped with thirty such virgin
tablets, and I've laid in other essentials, too. A box of Bic pens,
a carton of filter-tipped Camels, a jar of Maxwell House instant coffee with a submersible heating coil, two pastrami
sandwiches from room service, a liter of amontillado in a nov-
elty cut-glass decanter. This is Edgar Allan Poe's city, after all,
and I've decided to pay him homage. Pardon me while I take
a few sips of sherry — yes, it's decadent to drink before noon,
but Poe's hovering shade expects me to follow protocol — and
then I'll begin my tale.

At the moment I'm writing from the slough of despond, but
my mood was exultant and my career in full flower when the
two FBI agents showed up on the Monogram Pictures sound
stage to assess the caliber of my patriotism. We'd just finished
a productive morning's shoot on *Revenge of Corpuscula* for
dear old Sam Katzman and his noble little studio, William
Beaudine directing, Mack Stengler lensing, Dave Milton pro-
viding his usual bricks-without-straw décor. The screenplay
credit would go to Darlene, though I contributed six good lines
and two nifty plot twists during a furious forty-eight-hour rewrite session in our Santa Monica bungalow. Darlene and I
had been shacking up ever since falling head-over-heels on the
set of the original *Corpuscula*, which she wrote on a dare from
her best friend, Brenda Weisberg, the only woman in Hollywood routinely churning out horror movie scripts. (Brenda's

masterpiece is probably *The Mad Ghoul* of '43, though many fans swear by *The Mummy's Ghost* of two years later.) Oddly enough, Darlene's script was exactly what Sam had been looking for, and when the picture performed better than expected, he signed her to a six-year exclusive contract, an interval during which she was obligated to rewrite every crappy Bob Steele western and East Side Kids vehicle that landed on her desk, plus a gaggle of *Corpuscula* sequels.

Like the first three films in the cycle, all conspicuously profitable despite the constraints imposed by Monogram's accountants and the Second World War, *Revenge of Corpuscula* paired me with Siegfried K. Dagover, the latter playing Dr. Woltan Werdistratus to my hulking but articulate brute, Corpuscula. Darlene's ingenious variation on the Frankenstein myth had Werdistratus eschewing a mad scientist's normal method of creating artificial life: zapping a rag-doll assemblage of pilfered body parts with electricity. Instead, her insane doctor unearthed a human skeleton, using it as the matrix around which various organs, muscles, ligaments, vessels, and ducts coalesced by means of — and here Darlene was exploiting a motif from Mary Shelley's original novel — alchemical procedures pioneered by Paracelsus and his fellow adepts. About five years ago the master's theses started appearing, bearing titles like "Hollywood's Challenge to Empiricism's Hegemony: Magic and Medicine in the Corpuscula Cycle." You think I'm kidding.

We'd gotten it in the can, by God, the three most difficult pages in Darlene's script, Corpuscula threatening to hand Dr.

Werdistratus over to the authorities unless the two of them reach an understanding. If you've seen the picture, you remember the routine, the alchemical monster strapping his creator to a torture rack in the dungeon laboratory, then confronting him with a cavalcade of pickled brains, each belonging to a recently deceased genius, the monster's aim being for Werdistratus to fuse them into a supercerebrum and graft it onto Corpuscula's cortex, thereby transforming him from outcast to intellectual giant. As usual, Dagover tried to hijack the scene, and as usual I didn't let him. He wasn't a terrible actor, but he had only two personae: neurasthenic connoisseur of the dark arts, and deranged desecrator of God's designs. I could act him under the table with a paper bag over my head and a clothespin on my tongue.

Beyond our successful rendering of the torture rack scene, I had other reasons to be jubilant. The previous morning, Darlene's pregnancy test had come back negative. Two days earlier, Germany had surrendered unconditionally to the Allies. And to top it off, at the beginning of the week I'd finished my first serious attempt at screenwriting. In my opinion *Lycanthropus* was so scary it made Siodmak's script for *The Wolf Man* seem like a bedtime story for depressive children, though I wouldn't be truly pleased with my achievement until Darlene told me it was swell.

With Beaudine's blessing Dudley the AD decreed a lunch break, saying he wanted everybody back at 1:30 P.M. sharp on stage two for the big cemetery scene — Werdistratus and his warpie assistant, Klorg, skulking among the graves with spades, prospecting for carrion — and then the pair of G-Men came striding across the laboratory set, hopscotching among the cables and gobo stands, outfitted in genuine Lamont Cranston slouch hats and *misterioso* sunglasses. At first I thought they were actors themselves, headed for the nearest exit after appearing in some dopey spy thriller on stage three, but when they brushed up against me, tugged on my sheepskin doublet, and hustled me into a fretwork of *film noir* shadows, I realized they had something else in mind. They introduced themselves as Agent Jones and Agent Brown — their real names, I later learned, though at the time I didn't believe them. The grilling began instantly, before I could remove a shred of makeup. Corpuscula gave them no pause, despite the third eye embedded in his cheek and the herniated brain emerging from his fractured skull. I figured such *sang-froid* was habitual for guys in their line. The rest of the day would probably find them coolly quizzing a bank robber as he lay expiring of gunshot wounds or calmly questioning a naked whore who'd just disemboweled a john in self-defense. A tattered ambulatory cadaver was nothing.

Agent Brown, a lardish man with a pencil-thin moustache, asked me if I was in fact "a Jew named Isaac Margolis who now calls himself Syms Thorley."

"Isaac was the name of a great uncle who died before I was born," I said, chattering nervously. I was convinced they'd come to arrest me as a draft dodger, even though I had a legitimate medical deferment. "It's a Jewish custom. You want to know anything else about my people, talk to Louis B. Mayer.

Being a Jew is not my area of expertise."

"Ah, so you're *assimilated*," said Agent Jones with an anti-Semitic curl of his lip. He had tiny eyes, bad teeth, and the negligible nose of an altar-boy Pinocchio.

"My *bubbe* keeps trying to make me observant," I said, "but all I really care about is the movies."

"That fits with the data we've collected so far," Agent Brown said.

"Did my draft board send you here?" I asked. "I'm classified 1-M."

"We know all about your flat feet," Agent Jones said. "A mighty fortunate handicap, if you ask me."

"We also know about last summer's appendectomy and your girlfriend's pregnancy test," Agent Brown said.

"Here's the deal, Thorley," Agent Jones said. "Your Uncle Isaac might be dead, but your Uncle Sam is alive and kicking, and he's got a special assignment for you, something any red-blooded, stouthearted, flat-footed American would be keen to take on."

Just then Dagover strolled by, still in character, the wild-eyed Werdistratus, obviously hoping I'd gotten in trouble and eager to overhear the details.

"We need to take this conversation elsewhere," Agent Brown said, casting a suspicious eye on the mad scientist.

"I'm afraid Monogram doesn't have a commissary, but there's a swell little Mexican place on the corner of Sunset and Talmadge," I said.

"The Neon Cactus," Agent Jones said, nodding.

"We've reserved a booth," Agent Brown said.

"Hey, Dudley," I called to the AD, "Eliot Ness and his transvestite sister are taking me out to lunch. I'm done for the day, right?"

Dudley flipped open his brass-handled board. "No more Corpuscula scenes this afternoon, but we need you in your makeup for an 8:00 A.M. take one. Do me a favor and be at the studio by six."

"Here's an idea," I told Dudley. "Have Carl come out to my house at dawn tomorrow and put the makeup on me while I'm still asleep."

"I hate this job," Dudley said.

"A bewildered Syms Thorley and his new friends set off for the Neon Cactus, in quest of whatever's on tap," I said, flashing the AD a florid Corpuscula grin. "Fade-out."

What they had on tap was Dos Equis, which the G-Men and I supplemented with outsized orders of tacos and gazpacho. Actors and soldiers jammed the place to the walls. A lively lass with a pretty face and a considerable figure brought us our food. The cliché is true now, and it was true then: L.A. has the most nubile waitresses in the world, hopeful starlets anticipating the proper cosmic conjunction of a cruising producer and a flattering sunbeam.

My makeup was itching, so I tugged at the latex appliance, pulling a huge swatch from my forehead along with my fright wig, then set the hairy puddle beside me on the bench. I removed my third eye and the dentures, resting them atop the napkin dispenser. My behavior attracted no attention. This was Hollywood. In the next booth over, the Abominable Snowman drank a vanilla milkshake through a straw. Napoleon sat at the counter, munching on a doughnut. Beside the swinging doors to the kitchen, Julius Caesar was propositioning our waitress.

"Uncle Sam doesn't want you in uniform, but he *does* want you in a suit," Agent Jones told me.

"A clown suit?" I said. "I'm supposed to tour the Pacific with the USO, cheering up the troops? I don't do clowns, only monsters."

"That's exactly the idea," Agent Brown said. "Uncle Sam wants you in a monster suit. Nick and I have to decide if you're a security risk. We're also supposed to soften you up."

"With your fists?"

"With the news that the assignment pays ten thousand dollars."

"Ten thousand? Jeez."

"Personally, I think you should do it out of sheer bare-assed patriotism," Agent Jones said, "especially since you're so assimilated and everything."

"To tell you the truth, we were thinking of recommending your co-star Dagover, but the Navy seems to think you're the better actor," Agent Brown said.

"The Navy knows what they're talking about," I said.

Let me take this opportunity to set the record straight. There was no rivalry between Siggy Dagover and myself. There was, rather, an unimaginably vicious vendetta that stopped short of

homicide only because in Hollywood there are more imagina-
tive ways to settle scores. Think of Joan Crawford versus Bette
Davis, and you'll have some idea of the scale involved.

The only thing I admired about Dagover was his ambition.
Hired by Göttingen University as a linguistics professor way
back in '34, he became the first Gentile intellectual on his block
to flee Hitler. Landing in Manhattan as the Great Depression
was reaching its nadir, he briefly supported himself by washing windows and scrubbing floors for the few remaining pluto-
crats in New York, then hopped a series of freight trains for the
coast, determined to bluster his way into the movies.

"Any Japs up your family tree?" Agent Jones asked me
abruptly.

"Only moneylenders, bagelmakers, and rabbis," I said, not
really expecting a laugh. Humor was never the strong suit of
anti-Semites, except when T. S. Eliot wrote about cats.

"That accords with our findings," Agent Jones said.

"What associations does the name Karl Marx bring to
mind?" Agent Brown asked.

"I believe he stayed in New York with Gummo when the
others went out West," I said.

"Are you prepared to sign a loyalty oath?" Agent Brown
asked.

"To which country?" I asked.

"I have infinite patience," Agent Jones said. "I really do. My
patience goes from here to the goddamn moon."

"This woman you're living with, Darlene Wasserman,
did you know her parents once belonged to the Communist

League?" Agent Brown asked. "Your girlfriend was a red-diaper baby."

"I thought we were fighting Hirohito this week, not Stalin."

"Tell me about Miss Wasserman's politics."

"She voted for Roosevelt, just like everybody else," I said.

"What about you?" Agent Jones said.

"If I ever run for president, I'm sure Darlene will vote for me."

"Did *you* vote for Roosevelt?"

"I don't remember."

"According to our investigations, you and Miss Wasserman are registered Democrats."

"That's completely correct. Our diapers are as white as yours, Nick."

"One more crack, Jew-boy, and the job goes to Dagover," Agent Jones said.

"Why does Uncle Sam want me in a monster suit?" I asked.

"We can't tell you that," Agent Brown said.

"Because you aren't allowed, because you don't know, or because you despise me?" I asked.

"We can't tell you that either," Agent Brown said.

"Actually, I'd be happy to address your third question," Agent Jones said.

Agent Brown passed me a slip of paper bearing the words *4091 East Olympic Boulevard, Room 101, 0900 Hours*. "Show up at this address tomorrow morning, nine o'clock sharp."

"With my monster makeup on, or without it?" I asked, removing the fake eye from the napkin dispenser. Dudley would be miserable about this latest hitch in the schedule, but that was the price you paid for trying to make horror movies during a global conflagration.

"Tell them you're the actor, come to see Commander Quimby," Agent Jones said.

"Bombs over Tokyo," I said, nonchalantly dropping my glass orb into the G-Man's gazpacho. "Look, Nick, there's an eye in your soup. If you don't make a big deal about it, I'm sure they'll bring you a fresh bowl."

That night I made a pot of spaghetti for Darlene and myself, then read her the first draft of *Lycanthropus*, insisting that she should feel perfectly free to give me her frank professional opinion leavened with unqualified adulation. Three or four lines went clunk, and for budget purposes I'd probably have to cut the prologue set in ancient Rome, but basically I had to agree with her when she said the thing was a whiz-bang, gosh-wow masterpiece.

"It's too good for Katzman," she elaborated, puffing on a postprandial Chesterfield. She was the sort of creature a down-market writer might describe as "a mere slip of a girl," though I found her ethereality wholly sensual and paradoxically carnal. "You've got to peddle it to Warners or Universal."

"Universal would let me keep ancient Rome," I said.

"You know what you've got here, Syms? A goddamn series, that's what. *Curse of Lycanthropus*, *Chutzpah of Lycanthropus*, *Boston Blackie Meets Lycanthropus* — it's all sewn up."

I thought she was being too optimistic, but I would say one

thing for my script: whatever its flaws, I doubted that any-body had treated werewolfery in quite this way before. Unlike Henry Hull's neurotic Dr. Glendon or Lon Chaney, Jr.'s self-pitying Larry Talbot, my aristocratic scientist Baron Basil Or-dlust actually *wanted* to be a shapeshifter. Convinced that ly-canthropy offers the ultimate thrill, promising the one perver-sion that could sate his rarefied appetites, Ordlust travels the world seeking carriers of the supreme lupine curse — might he find the quintessential beast in Rumania? Russia? Cambodia? Tibet? Brazil? — soliciting these princely werewolves to plant their teeth judiciously in his flesh. Although most of the in-fections take hold, the subsequent transformations always fall short of Ordlust's expectations, so he blithely cures himself and hits the road once again, still seeking the ultimate in me-phistophelean saliva. And to top it off, Ordlust is a *sympathetic* character.

A word about the culture of Hollywood horror actors, circa 1945. You might be surprised to learn that our proud little fra-ternity had no particular affection for hideous makeup, even though deformity was the *sine qua non* of the genre. Sure, I suppose the elder Lon Chaney reveled in his masochistic man-of-a-thousand-faces mystique, but the rest of us had other agendas. Fanged dentures, itinerant eyeballs, gaping nostrils, rubber humps on your back, stitches the size of football laces on your forehead — not only were such appliances painful, they tended to cramp your performance. If you couldn't arrange to get cast as a vampire or a psychopath, you at least wanted a character who oscillated between a mute monster and a loquacious man. That's why the werewolf was such a coveted role within my profession. The fuzzy discomfort would be over in three or four shooting days, and then you'd get to deliver lots of dialogue, usually the best lines in the script. Mummies were a dicier proposition. Karloff famously had it both ways when he played Im-Ho-Tep back in '32. He's trussed up in those damn bandages for only about three minutes of screen time, first in the great resurrection scene, then briefly during the lavish flashbacks set in ancient Egypt. For most of the picture he's Ardeth Bey, unraveled mummy, a bit dry to the touch but smoothly lisping his way through one tasty line after another. I enjoyed no such luck with the Kha-Ton-Ra cycle. The scripts had me embalmed in every shot, though I got to do some pretty adept pantomime in *Bride of Kha-Ton-Ra* and *Ghost of Kha-Ton-Ra*. So *Lycanthropus* was a dream project for me, seventy-two discrete speeches ranging from pseudo-Shakespearean bombast to Oscar Wildean epigrams.

At first Darlene wanted to accompany me to Commander Quimby's lair, but then I explained how touchy my prospective employers were about national security, and why showing up with the spawn of Trotskyites on my arm might throw the Navy for a loop.

"My red diapers are behind me," she said, deadpan. In those days, even when Darlene's jokes weren't funny, I laughed.

"How's this for a deal?" I said. "Stay home today, but if Uncle Sam needs a rewrite on this mysterious script of his, I'll try to get you the job."

Appeased, Darlene promised to spend the morning ornamenting *Lycanthropus* with constructive criticism, then sent me off with a hug and a kiss.

4091 East Olympic Boulevard proved to be a nondescript one-storey sandstone building of the sort you drive blithely by every day, knowing it's full of paper-pushers and clock-watchers, and nobody's in there writing a symphony or taming a lion or having an orgasm. I parked around the corner, availed myself of the side entrance, and strolled into Room 101, its door framing a pane of frosted glass stenciled with the words *New Amsterdam Project, Los Angeles Office, No Admittance*. A buxom brunette in a WAVES uniform stepped out from behind the counter, a little plaque reading *Lt. Percy* pinned on her left jalookie. Learning that I was the expected movie star, she guided me down a stairwell, through a door marked *Interrogation Room*, and into the august presence of Commander Quimby, a gaunt officer in dress blues and a frothy auburn toupee that surmounted his cranium like a thatched roof.

I saluted. Quimby frowned, evidently wondering if I might be mocking him. I was wondering the same thing.

"I'll put my cards on the table, Thorley," he said as Lieutenant Percy slipped away. "The FBI thinks you're a smart-aleck, and they told us that Karloff, Dagover, or even Lorre might work out better."

"Peter could never get a security clearance," I said. "He's a double risk — born a Kraut, and before the war he played Mr. Moto."

"I just got off the phone with the State Department. Jimmy

Byrnes's people are satisfied you're true blue, plus you have the necessary stamina, or so your doctor told Jones and Brown."

"I heard I'm getting ten thousand dollars."

"Correct, but you'd be obliged to sign the contract even if the job paid fifty cents. Next week you've got a briefing at a secret military installation. The rehearsal comes nine or ten days later. We've decided to let you keep on working at Monogram, so your colleagues won't get suspicious, but every time we snap our fingers, you'll have to drop what you're doing and get on the Navy's clock."

"Mr. Katzman won't like that."

"Mr. Katzman can kiss my ass. The curtain goes up at 1500 hours on the first Sunday in June, one performance only, after which you can go back to *Corpuscula Humps the Wolf Man* without any more interruptions."

"Why just one show?"

"You don't need to know that yet."

"Who's the audience?"

"You don't need to know that yet either."

"Do I have any lines?"

"Ten thousand dollars for three days' work, and you're worried about your goddamn *lines?*"

"I'm always worried about my goddamn lines."

Quimby issued a polysyllabic grunt, opened his desk drawer, and took out a neatly folded American flag along with a dossier labeled *Syms Thorley*. "I've got your contract right here, three copies, plus a loyalty oath, a level three security clearance, and an ID badge that will get you admitted to certain sectors of the project."

"I can't sign anything today. Not before my agent reads it over."

"Fuck your agent. This is your contribution to the *war effort*, Thorley, not a goddamn career move." Quimby plucked the fountain pen from his desk set, flipped open the dossier, and retrieved the specified documents, sliding them toward me with the revulsion of a gourmet chef serving a cheeseburger. "Put your right hand on Old Glory," he said, indicating the folded flag, "and repeat after me, 'I, Isaac Margolis, swear my undying allegiance to the Constitution of the United States...'"

I froze, mulling over the word *undying*. Three years earlier, a quirky little werewolf picture called *The Undying Monster* had turned a tidy profit for Fox, a circumstance that I thought boded well for *Lycanthropus*.

"Say it, Thorley," Quimby insisted, "or we open negotiations with Dagover."

I gave the flag a patriotic caress. "'I, Isaac Margolis, swear my undying allegiance to the Constitution of the United States...'"

"'And I shall spare myself no hazard or hardship in defending the republic against its enemies.'"

"That, too." I grabbed the fountain pen and scrawled my name on every dotted line in sight.

Quimby heaved a sigh of relief, then got on the intercom and told somebody named "Ensign Fuentes" I was ready to have my measurements taken. The commander jammed two contracts back into my dossier, along with the loyalty oath and the security clearance, then presented me with the remaining contract plus an ID badge announcing that Syms Thorley was a civilian attaché to the New Amsterdam Project of the United States Navy, Group F, Classification C, Serial Number 873091.

"I have about six hundred questions for you," I said.

"And I've got exactly six answers for you."

"I'll take them."

"Nothing I'm about to say leaves this room. Don't even tell your girlfriend."

"You bet." I couldn't wait to regale Darlene with a complete account of this bizarre interrogation.

"First answer. The New Amsterdam Project is actually the code name for the Knickerbocker Project. If your friends at Monogram insist on hearing any details, tell them you've been hired by the New Amsterdam Project. Mention the words 'Knickerbocker Project,' and the Navy will shoot you on sight."

"I see," I said between clenched teeth.

"Second answer. The Japs are licked. The President knows it, the Army knows it, the Navy knows it, and even His Divine Goddamn Majesty Hirohito knows it. Third answer. Those little yellow bastards would rather arm their grandmothers with bamboo spears than hand their flag to an Allied invasion force, so the Joint Chiefs have been casting around for a way to shock them into unconditional surrender. Even as we speak, General Groves is riding herd on some goddamn *Astounding Science Fiction* superbomb that Leo Szilard and his nutcase physics friends started building after FDR gave them the green light. Meanwhile, Admiral Strickland is supervising a program aimed at developing the ultimate biological weapon, just like the Nazis were working on before Hitler killed himself. It's funny, Szilard is an anagram for lizards, but the *Navy's* the ones with the lizards, not the Army."

"Did you say lizards?"

I was hoping Ensign Fuentes would turn out to be a WAVE, just like Lieutenant Percy, but the officer who came barreling into the room was a hulking Wallace Beery lookalike with no neck, a wooden pencil lodged behind his cauliflower ear and a Masonite clipboard tucked under his arm. A yellow cloth tape measure hung from his shoulders like a tallith. He set to work immediately, assessing my height, determining my circumference, establishing the distance from my left shoulder to my right.

"No, Thorley, I did not say lizards," Quimby explained as Fuentes wrote down his findings. "You merely *thought* I said lizards. Fourth answer. The instant we relay your measurements to the costumers, they can finish constructing your PRR."

"Pennsylvania Railroad?"

"Personal Reptile Rig."

Fuentes systematically ascertained and recorded the dimensions of my head, neck, chest, and hips.

"Fifth answer," Quimby said. "Once we process the paperwork, you'll be seconded to the staff of Dr. Ivan Groelish, Nobel laureate, herpetologist, and all-around odd duck. Expect a phone call from him, possibly his daughter, on Monday."

"A herpetologist," I said. "A lizard man."

"Sixth and final answer. Don't be fooled by Dr. Groelish's civilian status. You're working for the United States Navy, not the goddamn private sector. If it were up to me, I'd draft you into the Pacific Fleet tomorrow."

Fuentes carefully calculated the lengths of my arms, legs, and stride.

"Let's be honest, Commander," I said. "For reasons not remotely clear to me, and perhaps not to you either, these Knickerbocker people are planning to put me in a lizard suit."

Quimby rifled through my dossier, then yanked out a one-page letter. "You want to know why we're having this conversation? Dr. Groelish's plea arrived on my desk yesterday. Quote, 'The USO finally managed to dig up those 16mm prints, so last night we had a private Syms Thorley festival, attended by most of the Group F personnel and also Admiral Yordan. Please do whatever it takes to get Mr. Thorley on the team. The man is a consummate shambler. Screen *Return of Kha-Ton-Ra*, and you'll see what we mean. His lumbering is second to none. If you doubt this evaluation, take a look at *Evil of Corpuscula*.' Unquote."

"In my opinion, everything Dr. Groelish says is true," piped up Fuentes. "I was only nine when I saw *Return of Kha-Ton-Ra*, and I still get the heebie-jeebies just thinking about it. May I shake your hand, Mr. Thorley?"

"Of course," I said, granting my admirer's wish. "They want me to be a lizard, right?"

"I'm not at liberty," the ensign said. "Now may I ask *you* a question?"

"You bet."

"Did you play both parts in *Corpuscula Meets the Doppel-gänger*?"

It was actually the first time anyone had ever asked me that, and I was pleased to set him straight.

"What do you think?" I said.

"It had to be you in both cases. There's only one Syms Thorley."

"Good answer, Mr. Fuentes. Tell the costumers I want plenty of ventilation. When I played the robot in *Flesh of Iron*, I practically died of heatstroke."

II

AMONG THE BETTER Edgar Allan Poe stories nobody reads anymore is "MS. Found in a Bottle," a metaphysical adventure that Roger Corman once considered adding to his famous cycle of Poe adaptations. I know this because Roger approached me about playing the lead. Negotiations broke off for several reasons, including my casual remark, "So why aren't you using Vincent again? Did a piece of undigested scenery from *Pit and the Pendulum* give him dyspepsia?" While the title might lead you to expect a story about a mad embalmer who specializes in feminists, "MS. Found in a Bottle" is in fact a morbid and ambiguous nautical tale concerning a shipwrecked *flâneur* and his gradual realization that heaven and earth hold more things than are dreamt of in his skepticism. Had Corman actually made the picture, I'm sure that his patron corporation, American-International, aghast at the uncommercial title, would have pulled a variation on the bait-and-switch they used when releasing *The Conqueror Worm* and *The Haunted Palace*, allegedly based on the corresponding Poe poems but actually derived from non-Poe sources, a Ronald Bassett novel called *Witchfinder General* in the first instance and H. P. Lovecraft's *The Colour Out of Space* in the second. I know that Corman and his screenwriters intended to retain most of the key story elements from "MS. Found in a Bottle" — the black ship, its spectral crew, the Polar whirlpool — but the picture would still have been billed as "Edgar Allan Poe's *The Imp of the Perverse*" or "Edgar Allan Poe's *The Descent into the Maelstrom*" or "Edgar Allan Poe's *Spirits of the Dead*" or whatever fan-friendly Poe title was still lying around.

The present memoir is not so much a manuscript found in a bottle as one poured from a decanter. Thanks to a few golden ounces of amontillado — "For the love of God, Montresor!" — I've managed to scrawl my way through an entire legal pad in only three hours. After I replenish my glass and take a few swallows, I'll tell you about my big meeting with the whack-jobs who ran the Knickerbocker Project.

Allow me to clarify my earlier remark concerning vampires. While it's true that Count Dracula and his undead brethren were once supreme among the roles preferred by horror per-formers, I myself always refused to don the cape and fangs. This gap in my résumé traces to a promise I once made my maternal grandmother, who, upon resigning herself to the fact that I would probably spend the rest of my life portray-ing movie monsters, told me, "No vampires, Isaac. Our people have spent a hundred generations running away from crosses, and I won't have you doing the same." I'm proud to say I've remained true to my *bubbe*, even to the point of turning down the role of the blood-drinking cucumber in Corman's drive-in classic, *Demon from Beyond the Stars*.

Shortly after writing about dropping the eye in Agent Jones's gazpacho, I started fiddling absent-mindedly with the channel changer on my Holiday Inn TV. I soon stumbled upon the big news of the day, a survey suggesting that come November President Reagan — dear old Ronnie, that former friend of the working man, famously sympathetic to the carpenters' strike that rocked Hollywood back when we were shooting *Revenge of Corpuscula* — will clobber Walter Mondale at the polls. Next I tuned in the nascent cable channel called American Movie Classics, and you'll never guess what they were running. No, not a Corpuscula picture, something far more interesting, *Trumpet Voluntary*, 1936, directed by Lewis Milestone, the absorbing saga of two families, one rich, one poor, anticipating their sons' return from the trenches of the Great War, screenplay by my cynical, resentful, intermittently lamented father. Although the late Nathan Margolis and I never really got along, I continue to admire the way that, as a contract writer first for Paramount, later for Warners and MGM, he occasionally got himself attached to a serious drama, as opposed to the reliably profitable stuff the studios preferred to make — the musicals, screwball comedies, Shirley Temple vehicles, horror pictures, gangster movies: Hollywood's elixir for the Great Depression. Besides *Trumpet Voluntary*, Nathan scripted *Mickey O'Neil's Favorite Planet*, that piquant Frank Capra parable, which nobody went to see, about a New York cop who wins the Irish Sweepstakes, then tries in vain to make the world a better place, as well as the equally unprofitable *Adventures of Charles Darwin*, Mervyn LeRoy at the helm, a well-researched bio-pic about the uneventful life of the unassuming Englishman who undermined — and what kind of assignment was this for a Jewish boy? — the Torah's account of human origins.

My father lost no opportunity to tutor me in his philosophy of screenwriting. His words of wisdom still ring in my ears. "There are only three rules, Isaac. Never let a dog die on screen. Never advance the plot by having somebody say, 'Why are you telling me this?' And never have a character commit suicide. Beyond that, it's deuces wild." I'm proud to say that I obeyed my father's commandments not only when composing my *Lycanthropus* script but also in conducting my personal affairs. Of course, *The Syms Thorley Story* is not yet completely written, but I see no defunct canines on the horizon, and the same goes for conveniently curious characters.

We'd just wrapped the first of the three big orangutan scenes in *Revenge of Corpuscula* when Trixie the stenographer came trotting across stage three with the news that "a vitally urgent phone call, but that's what they all say" was waiting for me in Mr. Katzman's office.

The morning's shoot had not gone well. On paper the scene looked simple enough. Corpuscula breaks into Dr. Werdistratus's lab intending to steal his journal, but then he notices the mad scientist's pet orangutan, Bongowi, caged in the corner, so he decides to steal the animal instead. Sam had insisted we use a live ape, on the dubious theory that it would be cheaper than renting a suit and paying some bit player scale to wear it, but the people at Celluloid Critters had failed to train the wretched beast properly.

"Werdistratus is not the only surgeon in Europe," I tell the kidnapped Bongowi. "Somehow I shall persuade Dr. Niemuller to implant carnivorous impulses in your brain, then send you off to kill your master."

After delivering the line, I merely had to open the cage and lead Bongowi away by the handy collar Werdistratus had placed around his neck. Unfortunately the damn orangutan was suffering from some kind of primate depression, because he slouched in the back of the cage and wouldn't budge, no matter how hard I tugged on the chain. His handler was apologetic, and a lot of good that did us. Eventually Beaudine resorted to giving an apprehensive gaffer five dollars to jab a fork into Bongowi's rump, with Stengler framing the shot so tightly the audience would never know.

Beaudine decided to accompany me to the front office, since he wanted to have a word or two with Katzman concerning the orangutan fiasco. Trixie handed me the phone. While I spoke in my most patriotic whisper to a reedy-voiced woman who identified herself as Joy Groelish, daughter of the Project Director and a biologist in her own right, Katzman and Beaudine exchanged heated words about the melancholic Bongowi.

"Do you still live at 1901 Marguerita Avenue, Santa Monica?" Joy asked me.

"Indeed."

"That hairy cocksucker's a loser, Sam," Beaudine said. "He just sits there and stares into space."

"I'm your official liaison to the Knickerbocker Project," Joy said.

"I've had liaisons before," I told her, "but never an official one."

"We have to replace him," Beaudine said.

"Impossible," Katzman said. "Celluloid Critters is fresh out of primates."

"I mean replace him with an actor in a suit," Beaudine said.

"I'll pick you up tomorrow at 7:00 A.M. sharp," Joy said.

"Sure thing," I said.

"Dress for hot weather. Destination Mojave. Don't forget your ID badge. Toodle-oo."

"Good-bye," I said.

"Orangutan suits are expensive," Katzman said.

"So are movie directors," Beaudine said. "I've had it, Sam. It's hard enough trying to keep Thorley and Dagover in line, and now this ape shit. If you have to hire Ollie Drake to finish *Revenge*, he'll end up working overtime getting ready to shoot *Lonesome Trail*. The union'll come after you."

"Gentlemen, I have a suggestion," I said, setting the receiver back in its cradle. "Why don't we all take tomorrow off and spend the day making an orangutan suit?"

"Are you crazy?" Beaudine said.

"Fuck that," Katzman said.

"I'll give it to you straight," I said. "I just learned that, first thing in the morning, I'm off to a secret U.S. Navy installation in the desert."

"Like hell you are," Beaudine said. "You're taking that goddamn ape to Dr. Niemuller so he can turn it into a carnivore."

"The desert?" said Katzman. "The last I heard, the Navy was

a seagoing operation."

"I'm perfectly serious," I said, flourishing my New Amsterdam Project ID badge. "On Friday I signed a government contract." I went on to explain that, for reasons not yet clear to me, the war effort required my acting skills. I told them I was obligated to attend tomorrow's briefing, then a rehearsal the following week, but the show itself would be closing after one Sunday matinee, so there was every reason to believe we could still bring *Revenge* in on time.

"What the hell is the New Amsterdam Project?" Beaudine asked.

"The code name for the Daffy Duck Project," I said.

"You signed a fucking contract without telling me?" Katzman said, seething.

"It's all very hush-hush," I said. "You'll have to shoot around me. I hate to dick with the schedule, but Uncle Sam needs me, and there's really no choice."

"Syms may actually have a decent idea there," Beaudine told Katzman. "I'll get Dudley to shuffle the call sheets, and tomorrow we'll shoot Werdistratus strangling Klorg and maybe also the madhouse scene, and meanwhile Trixie can hunt up a cheap orangutan suit. My brother-in-law will play the part. He owes me a big favor, so he'll do it for nothing. Can the budget handle nothing at this point, Sam?"

"I want to see this government contract of yours," Katzman informed me.

"I'll have Darlene bring it around tomorrow," I said.

"When you get back to the set, tell that Celluloid Critters

bozo to come in here, dragging his Bongowi behind him,"
Katzman instructed Beaudine. "I want the pleasure of firing
that fucking monkey in person."

If you're a connoisseur of post-war science fiction films, with
their mutant insects, outsized octopi, defrosted dinosaurs,
and piscine horrors rising from opaque lagoons, you know
that the writers repeatedly employed a conceit that, in retro-
spect, seems to strike a blow for feminism. Because the audience presumably expected a love interest — though I don't
think the children who actually went to see these pictures were
ever consulted in the matter — the male protagonist's quest
to outwit the monster often found him collaborating with a
beautiful lady scientist, sometimes the daughter of the dotty
old entomologist or paleontologist charged with identifying
the menace in question, sometimes simply a career girl with
a PH.D., her urge to decipher nature's secrets having brought
her on board whatever research project had inadvertently
spawned, unearthed, thawed, annoyed, or lured the beast.
As any film historian will tell you, there are more sharp and
savvy females per capita in 1950's sci-fi cinema than in all other
genres combined.

Ivan Groelish's daughter was not beautiful, but she radiated
a kind of cerebral sensuality — the ineffable eroticism of intel-
lect — that rendered her knobby chin, droopy eyes, and equiv-
ocal lips moot. The farther we got out of the city, Joy driving
her '39 Chevy convertible at a treacherous seventy-five MPH
along a crumbling stretch of two-lane blacktop that would one

day transmute into the Antelope Freeway, the more smitten I became. As my high-browed, ovum-domed companion spoke of how Mendelian genetics had revolutionized the field of selective breeding, a subject about which I knew nothing and still do, my heart became crammed to bursting with lascivious sentiments, and I winced internally when she mentioned her engagement to a chemistry professor at the University of San Diego. Owing to Joy's knowledge of organic molecules and other carnal entities, my emotional infidelity to Darlene persisted throughout the day and many more days to come, a betrayal that I now confess only in light of Poe's epigraph to "MS. Found in a Bottle," a quotation from Phillip Quinault. *"Qui n'a plus qu'un moment a vivre n'a plus rien a dissimuler."* He who has but a moment to live has nothing more to hide.

We followed Route 14 north through the simmering sands, past the crimson cliffs of Red Rock Canyon, chatting all the while about the trundling mummies and hobbling zombies that had brought my talents to the attention of the Knickerbocker Project. Reaching Route 78, my liaison hooked a right and headed west, racing the Mojave wind to a negligible settlement called Inyokern, where we ordered lunch at the solitary café. We swilled our black coffee, gobbled our wieners, returned to the convertible, and, zooming to the far side of town, encountered a barrage of signs instructing lost travelers to go get lost somewhere else.

CHINA LAKE NAVAL ORDNANCE TEST STATION:

RESTRICTED AREA

INYOKERN BIOLOGICAL WEAPONS

DEVELOPMENT FACILITY:

U.S. PERSONNEL ONLY

ARGUS RANGE RESEARCH CENTER:

KEEP OUT

For a horror actor with the proper security clearance, however, these admonitions meant nothing, and by flashing our ID
badges Joy and I successfully negotiated the subsequent suc-
cession of checkpoints, sentry boxes, crossing gates, perimeter
fences, and German shepherds.

While the China Lake Naval Ordnance Test Station was
ostensibly a military installation, under the impetus of the
Knickerbocker Project a civilian community had bloomed
within its bounds. In deference to the pedestrians, Joy slowed
down, cruising along Main Street at a mere forty MPH. Clusters of slapdash bungalows and prefabricated cottages rolled
by, their back yards filled with flotillas of laundry drying in
the desert air, the rows of monotonous dwellings interspersed
with playgrounds, tennis courts, and sandlot baseball fields.
Passing the limits of this *ad hoc* town, Joy once again hit the
accelerator, and we flew at full throttle down a sinuous dirt
road, a plume of dust and gravel billowing behind us like the
wake of a speedboat.

At last my liaison pulled up before a squat structure of
poured concrete buttressed with steel, bleak and featureless,
like a sepulcher for people who didn't believe in an afterlife.

The briefing bunker, Joy explained. Navy jeeps and staff cars jammed the parking lot. Spreading eastward from the gargantuan building was a vast stretch of water the color of a bruise. These days, of course, China Lake is dry as a mirage, but back then it was wet and deep. Clusters of bubbles bobbed and seethed just below the surface, as if the relentless sun were bringing the water to a boil.

Joy guided me through a reverberant vestibule and into an elevator car. Throughout our long and rapid descent my stomach issued frantic distress calls, while my throat constricted as if being squeezed by the clutching hand in Monogram's *Terror in the Green Room*, script by Darlene Wasserman. The next time this tidy little thriller comes on TV, take note of the bearded psychiatrist who shows up in the last scene, spouting the immortal line, "The human mind is deeper than the Mariana Trench." That's Sam Katzman himself, demonstrating to the world that he had every right to make a lot of cruddy B-movies, because he sure as hell couldn't act.

Although Joy had driven like a lunatic to get us to the meeting on time, we were still the last to arrive. Blue-uniformed Naval officers, white-coated biologists, and gray-faced eminences in charcoal suits filled the subterranean briefing room, everyone seated at a circular table that might have last seen service in some Paramount epic about King Arthur. Armed guards stood watch at all four corners. A fug of cigarette smoke hung in the air. Joy introduced me as "the man of the hour," then systematically presented my two dozen Knickerbocker colleagues, all of whose names I instantly forgot, with three exceptions: Rear Admiral George Yordan, my immediate sponsor, a spindly man with a black eye-patch, Vice Admiral Alexander Strickland, the blowzy Chief of Teratoid Operations, his face as flush and pliant as a hot-water bottle, and Joy's gnomish, dithery father, Dr. Ivan Groelish. The first time I met Lionel Atwill — at one of Siggy Dagover's famous parties, back before we'd learned to avoid each other everywhere except movie sets — I thought to myself, "Yes, this man is entirely capable of building an army of psychotic robots and setting them loose on the world," whereas Ivan Groelish looked barely capable of creating an unruly can opener.

The next ten minutes passed in stupefying small talk, during which interval a deferential sailor served us our choice of iced tea or hot coffee. A scowling commander whose name badge read *Barzak* informed me that his eleven-year-old son belonged to the Syms Thorley Fan Club, employing the same tone he might have used to confess that the boy smoked reefers. A sallow young biologist, Lance Pellegrino, complimented me on my performance in *Beyond the Veil*. Though a rationalist at heart, he could "not dismiss the possibility of life after death," and he thought I'd done a terrific job of "communicating what it's like to be a ghost." I told him that, though a romantic at heart, I did not believe in ghosts, "but, of course, if not for life after death, I'd be out of a job."

At last Admiral Strickland lit a Lucky Strike and, fixing me with the ineluctable stare of a professional basilisk, announced the start of the briefing. "For the sake of getting the best pos-

sible performance out of you, Mr. Thorley, we are about to dis-
close certain highly classified facts. Should you dare to reveal
them to another soul, including your paramour back in Santa
Monica — well, there's a word for that."

"Treason?" I ventured, sipping coffee.

"Bingo, Mr. Thorley. We could have you hanged."

"You don't say," I remarked as my stomach paid a second
visit to the descending elevator.

"Last week Commander Quimby informed you that our
mission here at China Lake has been to develop a unique variety of biological weapon, in tandem with the Army's efforts to
build a physics bomb," Dr. Groelish said in his alternately grav-
elly and squeaky voice. He sounded like a piccolo undergoing
puberty. "We shall now show you the fruits of our labors."

Two guards detached themselves from their niches and
activated a system of pulleys, thus causing a pair of crimson
drapes to part and reveal an enormous porthole framed by a
riveted brass ring, beyond which stretched the bottommost
reaches of the lake. Gasping and gaping, I surveyed the frothy
deep with its shoals of tuna, constellations of starfish, swarms
of eels, throngs of crabs, and three great underwater mountains. I felt like a guest on Captain Nemo's *Nautilus*.

"I wouldn't have guessed it's a saltwater lake," I said.

"It's not," Admiral Strickland explained. "The Seabees filled
the dry bed with brine."

"Where are the weapons?" I asked. "Are those tuna about to
explode?"

Dr. Groelish spread his arms in a gesture that encompassed

the whole of China Lake and all its imported inhabitants. "And the Voice from the Whirlwind spake unto Job, saying, 'Behold now behemoth, which I made with thee.'"

As if on cue, the three mountains trembled — they weren't mountains at all — stirring up blizzards of silt. What had roused the hellish beasts was not Dr. Groelish's biblical incantation but a courageous team of twenty Navy frogmen, gingerly approaching from the far shore. Feeding time at the end of the world, or so I surmised from the containers the divers were hauling, three immense steel cages abrim with shimmering fish.

"Our behemoths don't look especially ferocious now, but that's because they're heavily sedated," Commander Barzak noted.

Sedated or not, the monsters were ravenous. Inch by massive inch, yard by formidable yard, they struggled to stand erect, achieving a fully upright posture just as the cages floated within their grasp. The creatures suggested quarter-mile-high tyrannosaurs, but modified for a marine environment — pulsing gill slits, translucent swim fins, webbing between their talons like the vanes of a Spanish fan — and retrofitted with fighting tusks, barbed horns, feelers as long as tentacles, and dorsal plates the size and proportion of fir trees. Their eyes glowed like signal beacons relaying calamitous news. Their tails were reptiles unto themselves, great undulating sea serpents arrayed in thrusting spines. Hundreds of razor-sharp teeth crammed their jaws, shimmering through the swirling murk like columns supporting a temple consecrated to some unspeakable Lovecraftian god.

"The one with the bright red scales, that's Dagwood," Dr. Pellegrino informed me. "Beside him you see Blondie, with the blue stripes on her flanks, and over there we have Mr. Dithers, whose barbels are a hundred feet long."

"Our biggest challenge was figuring out how to induce accelerated maturation in common desert lizards, so we could breed them as rapidly as fruit flies," Dr. Groelish said. "Once we'd licked that problem, we knew the weapon would become a reality. Trace our behemoths back fifteen generations, and you'll encounter three innocuous iguanas."

Dagwood was the first to feast, seizing his portion of fish and stuffing the whole arrangement, cage and all, into his maw. As the monster bit down, the steel bars snapped like uncooked spaghetti. Next Blondie devoured her meal in one gulp, after which Mr. Dithers consumed his dragon chow. While the behemoths seemed to relish their lunches, I was on the point of relinquishing mine. There was nothing good about Dr. Groelish's monsters. These abominations should never have been born — born, synthesized, stitched together, alchemically confected, necromantically conjured, however they'd come into the world.

"Any one behemoth, acting on his own, could probably destroy a Japanese city in a matter of hours," Admiral Strickland said. "Just to be on the safe side, we plan to release them in teams of three."

"Dr. Groelish informs us that, besides Blondie, Dagwood, and Mr. Dithers, his team has twenty embryonic behemoths in the hatchery," Commander Barzak said. "There's never been an arsenal like this. We can thank our lucky stars that Hitler never got the lizard."

"One advantage of this weapon over conventional ordnance is that it doesn't require a delivery system," Strickland boasted. "No bombers needed, no rockets, no long-range cannons. We simply have to tow the sedated creature into Japanese coastal waters via submarine. As the tranquilizer wears off, we give the beast a colossal jolt of freedom by abruptly removing its shackles. This chain reaction now combines with the behemoth's instinctive viciousness to send it swimming to shore and rampaging across the countryside in search of a metropolis to incinerate."

"Incinerate?" I said. "They breathe fire?"

"Of course they breathe fire," Barzak said. "Why do you think they cost the taxpayers five hundred million dollars?"

"Next you'll be telling me they fly," I said.

"We looked into that," Dr. Pellegrino said.

"Bernoulli's principle shot us down," Dr. Groelish said.

"So, Mr. Thorley, what do you think?" Strickland asked.

"About what?"

"The Knickerbocker Project."

"You want my honest opinion?"

"Yes."

"Gentlemen, you are mad," I said.

"When we want your opinion, we'll ask for it," Barzak said.

"You're really going to set these horrors loose on civilian populations?" I tried to swallow more coffee but merely ended up gargling with it.

"Evidently you don't have any younger brothers in the Pacific right now, getting ready to invade Japan," Barzak said.

Now my liaison spoke up for the first time. "Personally, I'm glad the weapon makes Syms squeamish," Joy said. "That means his performance will be all the more sincere."

"Here's the deal, Mr. Thorley," Strickland said. "This past winter, after the Ardennes counteroffensive fell apart, it became clear that the European War would soon end, and by extension our lizard race with the Nazis. Sensing an opportunity, certain well-meaning biologists attached to the Knickerbocker Project, notably Dr. Groelish, plus a few high-minded Naval officers, notably Admiral Yordan, sent a petition to President Truman. They implored him to forbid biological sneak attacks against the Japanese."

"Instead, we advocated demonstrating the new weapon before an enemy delegation," Yordan said. "These witnesses would then, we hypothesized, convince the Imperial Government in Tokyo that capitulation was the best option."

"Sounds logical," I said.

"The problem is that Emperor Hirohito has always given his War Minister the last word in every political decision," Strickland said. "Rather than hand his sword to General MacArthur, General Anami would prefer to see every Nip man, woman, and child go down fighting."

"Come, come, Admiral," Dr. Groelish said. "Tokyo is burning, the Japanese navy's at the bottom of the sea, the blockade has brought famine, and the Russians are making noises about entering the Pacific Theater. A lizard demonstration should be all that's needed to make Hirohito stand up to Anami."

"A reasonable theory," I said.

"I didn't attend this meeting so I could hear some B-movie hambone give us his views on strategic doctrine," Barzak said.

"If it were up to me," Strickland said, pointing both extended index fingers in my direction like Bob Steele aiming his six-guns, "I'd clobber the enemy with Blondie and Dagwood right now and get it over with. Alas, it's not up to me. Ten days ago the President, having consulted with the Interim Committee of the Knickerbocker Project, cabled China Lake with his final decision. He wants us to try leveraging an unconditional Jap surrender through reptilian intimidation."

"Fortunately, we're prepared to carry out the President's orders," Dr. Groelish said. "Twenty-four hours after we mailed the China Lake Petition to Mr. Truman, Dr. Pellegrino and my daughter began laying the groundwork for a dramatic but bloodless behemoth demonstration, so that v-j Day might follow hard on the heels of v-e Day. Operation Fortune Cookie."

"Is that the code name," I asked, "or the code name's code name?"

"We already know you're a weisenheimer, Thorley," Barzak said. "It's in your dossier."

"We decided that in their present torpid state our mutant iguanas weren't going to scare anybody," Dr. Groelish said. "Yes, we could always remove the lizards from the lake and wake them up before a Japanese delegation, but if the animals subsequently went berserk, left the base, and attacked Los Angeles, the enemy would have the last laugh."

"Then the professor got a brainstorm," Yordan said. "Mr. Hilbert, let's go to the movies."

A lanky ensign rose from the briefing table, vanished through the rear door, and returned pushing a library cart holding a loaded Bell & Howell 16mm projector. As Hilbert plugged in the machine, another ensign marched across the room, grabbed a metal loop, and unscrolled a bright beaded screen.

"My idea was to breed a miniature form of the weapon," Dr. Groelish said. "With such a creature in hand, we could invite the enemy delegation into this room and show them Blondie, Dagwood, and Mr. Dithers. Later that same day, we would take the emissaries to Laboratory B and let them see our dwarf behemoths. The delegation's final stop would be an airplane hangar containing an elaborate scale model of an idealized Japanese city, which our most aggressive dwarf would proceed to stomp and burn before their eyes."

"One can easily imagine the psychological impact of such a demonstration," Dr. Pellegrino said. "The emissaries will go running to Hirohito, fall on their knees, and beg him to keep Japan from becoming the first casualty of the Lizard Age."

"Or so you imagine," Barzak said.

Ensign Hilbert switched on the projector, and a black-and-white image flickered across the screen: Joy standing in a gulch next to a dwarf behemoth. The creature was a perfect facsimile of Dagwood, with two nontrivial differences. He was barely a

foot taller than Joy, and there was nothing remotely intimidat-
ing about him. This lizard could not have demoralized a kitten
or frightened a squirrel up a tree, much less given a Japanese
diplomat the fantods. Just as the shot ended, the dwarf licked
Joy's cheek with his long moist tongue.

"I named him Rex," she said.

"As you can see, the Midget Lizard Initiative was a disaster," Dr. Groelish said. "For reasons we don't yet understand,
any juvenile version of a bipedal mutant iguana is completely
docile."

Jump-cut to Joy throwing a beach ball to another dwarf
behemoth. The monster bounced the ball off his knee, then
allowed it to settle on his snout. A circus seal could not have
performed the trick with greater dexterity.

"Her name is Evelyn," Joy said.

"Of course, we're still free to display our three midget lizards to the enemy delegation," Dr. Groelish said, "provided
we bend the truth a bit and insist that they're torpid because
they've been tranquilized — a safety precaution, we'll call it
— thus masking their congenital meekness."

"This is where you come in," Yordan said, fixing me with his
solitary eye. "In order for the Jap emissaries to end up witness-
ing a fire-breathing lizard wrecking our scale-model city, we'll
have to use an actor in a suit. If you can convince the delegation that you're midget lizard number four — that is, a real,
live, unsedated dwarf behemoth — and if you can destroy the
model with credible savagery, then we might, just might, pull
this bunny out of the bonnet."

I clicked my fingers nervously against my empty coffee mug, producing a series of brittle pings. "Performance as persuasion," I muttered.

"Exactly," Dr. Groelish said.

Jump-cut to yet another dwarf behemoth, paddling merrily across China Lake, Joy mounted on his back.

"We call him Oswald," she said.

"One complicating factor is that on Saturday the New Mexico team got some bad news," Yordan said. "There won't be enough weapons-grade uranium on the planet for at least a year."

"No physics bomb?" I asked.

Yordan nodded and said, "The President must now put all his eggs in the behemoth basket."

"Naturally we hope Operation Fortune Cookie gets the Japs crapping in their kimonos, but if it fails" — a Lugosian gleam entered both of Strickland's eyes — "Truman will have no choice but to deploy the lizards strategically."

"We don't want to put too much pressure on you, but it's essential that you understand the stakes," Yordan said. "Turn in a masterful performance, and the Pacific War may end happily."

"Screw it up, and we'll be forced to bust a Jap city or two," Strickland added.

Beads of sweat burst from my brow. Blood thumped in my ears. My breathing grew labored, as if I were back in my *Flesh of Iron* robot costume.

"I can't do it," I said.

"Of course you can," Yordan insisted.

"Don't be silly," Dr. Groelish chided me.

"We're counting on you," Dr. Pellegrino averred.

"You signed a contract," Strickland noted.

"I can't do it," I said again.

"Syms needs some fresh air," Joy told Strickland. "Let me take him topside. Once he clears the smoke out of his head, I'm sure he'll play ball."

"Forget it," I said.

"Syms, dear, we need to talk," Joy said.

"I can't do it."

By the time we'd finished the day's second elevator ride and stepped into the blaze of the Mojave sun, Joy had convinced me that I *could* do it — or, rather, that I *must* do it, because what other choice was there? Beyond Operation Fortune Cookie lay only two alternatives, both horrible: either a conventional invasion of the Japanese homeland, with innumerable casualties on both sides, or a full-scale behemoth attack on that same nation, with countless innocent civilians suffering immolation.

Admiral Yordan, Commander Barzak, and Dr. Groelish soon joined us on the broiling sands. "Mr. Thorley has seen the light," Joy told them.

"Up to a point, Admiral Strickland will be pleased," Barzak said, making an about-face and heading back to the briefing bunker.

Yordan guided us toward his staff car, where an acne-mottled sailor sat behind the wheel, looking eager to chauffeur his boss almost anywhere that wasn't the Pacific Theater.

"I'm confused," I said as we scrambled into the vehicle. "If the lizard demonstration comes a cropper, hasn't the United States lost the element of surprise?"

"That's a risk we're all happy to take," Dr. Groelish said.

"No, professor, it's a lesser evil we're all willing to tolerate," Yordan said.

"No, Admiral, it's a lesser evil *you're* willing to tolerate," Joy said. "You heard Strickland. He's hoping Truman will change his mind and unleash Blondie on Kyoto tomorrow."

Dr. Groelish told Yordan he needed to administer some nutrients to the twenty embryonic behemoths, and so our first stop become the main Knickerbocker laboratory, an imposing installation comprising a dozen interconnected domes rising from the sand like enormous beehives. A lurid billboard stood outside the facility, reminding the civilian scientists that academic freedom was not the norm at China Lake.

WHAT YOU SEE HERE
WHAT YOU HEAR HERE
WHAT YOU DO HERE
LET IT STAY HERE

We dropped off the mild-mannered monster-maker and continued our journey, speeding west past ranks of cacti and stands of acacia, eventually reaching an immense aluminum building labeled *Naval Ordnance Test Station: Hangar A*. Until six months ago, Yordan explained, the facility had been used to store and service Grumman F8F Bearcats and Consolidated PB4Y Privateers, but the Seabees had renovated the place top to bottom. Cecil B. DeMille, I decided, had nothing on the Pentagon. If the Navy wanted to transform an airplane hangar into a coliseum, put on a single apocalyptic matinee, then change the place back into a hangar, that's precisely what would happen.

The instant I stepped into the hot, cavernous structure, I felt right at home, for it immediately evoked a Monogram sound stage, though much bigger, large enough to accommodate not only a miniature facsimile of a major Japanese city sprawling across a raised platform — *Shirazuka, Island of Honshu*, according to the placard — but also a maze of catwalks outfitted with klieg lights and, suspended directly above the great model, a tier of stadium seating. Glass panels enclosed the posh balcony, presumably so the delegation would be spared the smoke, heat, and noise of Operation Fortune Cookie. For a full minute I simply stood and stared, wonderstruck at the hypothetical metropolis. Still under construction, it was easily the most astonishing *objet d'art* I'd ever seen, a sprawling expanse of factories, government buildings, office complexes, hotels, theaters, stores, apartments, temples, gardens, parks, and bridges, all decorated with signs and billboards beautifully lettered in kanji. Swathed in artificial clouds, a range of snow-capped peaks rose in the distance, the highest surmounted by the Imperial Palace. This was the sort of electric train set God's favorite cherubs got to play with — and among its marvels, in fact, was an O-gauge steam engine hauling a dozen coaches along a trestle-borne route running between the city and the hills. Besides the passenger train, the layout featured several locomotives pulling long strands of freight cars, plus an elaborate trolley system whisking its commuting patrons through downtown Shirazuka. Tiny barges plied the river. Toy merchant ships navigated the bay. Destroyers, cruisers, carriers, and a dreadnought lay moored in the harbor.

My awe was diminished only by the scores of craftsmen tiptoeing through the little city, their outsized bodies adding a touch of comical incongruity. A necessary invasion, for there were still many jobs to accomplish in the remaining weeks: painting buildings, paving roads, planting trees, hanging clouds, stringing telephone lines — each such operation being directed with great *élan* by a lively civilian foreman wearing jodhpurs and wielding a megaphone. How gratifying to see these legions of skilled Hollywood artisans in the Navy's gainful employ, especially since, owing to the carpenters' strike, most of them could no longer find paid work back at the studios.

"This is a masterpiece," I said.

"They're building another little city over in Hangar B," Joy explained. "Not an exact duplicate, much rougher, vulgar really — inferior materials, paper, cardboard, balsa wood, tin foil — but it'll do for the rehearsal."

"This way, Thorley," Yordan said, guiding me toward the harbor. A bronze chamber suggesting a bathyscaphe lay embedded in the bottom of the four-foot-deep pool. "The tank connects to the outside wall of the hangar. Before the Jap del-egation arrives, you'll pop the hatch on the dry side and climb into the compartment. As the curtain rises, you'll open the wet hatch and breach the surface."

"It will be the greatest entrance in the history of theater," Joy said, joining us by the bay. "A primordial dragon emerg-ing from the deep to spread chaos, panic, and pragmatism throughout Shirazuka."

I certainly wasn't expecting to meet anyone I knew, but I now recognized the foreman as a colleague: Willis O'Brien, who'd thrilled filmgoers with his stop-motion animation for the silent *Lost World* and, eight years later, *King Kong* — though, sad to say, he hadn't worked on any equally classy monster movies since. I imagine he detested *Son of Kong* no less than did the audiences who never went to see it.

"Mr. O'Brien?" I inquired tentatively.

The special-effects wizard cast me a skeptical glance. "Do I know you? Or, more to the point, am I *allowed* to know you?"

"He's allowed to know you, but he's not allowed to know what you know about Operation Fortune Cookie unless he al-ready knows it," Yordan explained. "And vice versa."

"Syms Thorley," I said, shaking the great man's hand.

"Call me Obie."

"We once met on a Sam Katzman set," I told him. "Mack Stengler had recruited you to help with the first shot of *Cor-puscula*. You were racking focus while the camera traveled toward your wonderful model of Castle Werdistratus. I had my monster makeup on, so you probably don't remember me."

"I was proud of that castle," Obie said. "We had birthday candles flickering in the windows."

"Is Castle Werdistratus the reason you got this job?" I asked.

"In truth it was *The Last Days of Pompeii*. God, what a lousy picture. Blacksmith gets perfect family, blacksmith loses perfect family, blacksmith finds Jesus, everybody dies. Ah, but my erupting Vesuvius, now *that* was something. Earthquakes reducing the temples to instant ruins. Fiery ash raining down from the skies. Two tons of steaming oatmeal gushing through the streets."

"I actually thought the Jesus stuff was pretty moving," I noted. Back then, we assimilated Jews said shit like that without even thinking about it.

"I can't blame you for missing my credit," Obie said. "'Chief technician Willis O'Brien' — what the hell is that supposed to mean? I wanted the card to read, 'Catechism by Jesus Christ. Cataclysm by Willis O'Brien.'" He turned to Joy and offered her a conspiratorial wink. "Don't tell me. Syms here is slated to play the lizard, right?"

Before she could answer, Yordan interposed his spidery frame between Joy and Obie. "Let's go over it once more, O'Brien. When a civilian drops by Hangar A, you can talk about three things: baseball, gas rationing, and the goddamn heat — period."

"Might I again make the case for using stop-motion instead of a sap in a suit?" Obie asked Yordan. "In three weeks the Lydecker boys could build you a scaled-down version of our Shirazuka miniature, and meanwhile Marcel and I will come up with an absolutely sensational behemoth model, fire-breathing, naturally, and with wings. Give me forty shooting days and a competent crew, and I'll deliver a spectacle that will make my Vesuvius explosion look like a fifth-grade science project."

"There isn't enough time," Yordan said.

"All right — two weeks for Babe and Ted to build the city, another two weeks for me to animate the scene," Obie said. "If you're worried about the budget, we'll do it in sixteen millimeter."

"The Jap emissaries have seen monster movies before. Maybe they've even seen *King Kong*. No, this has to be a *live* performance."

Obie sighed in resentful resignation, then faced Shirazuka and, raising his megaphone, issued an order to a hip-booted artisan standing knee-deep in the harbor. "The water's still not dark enough! This is the goddamn Jap Ragnarok, Buzzy! I want it to look like the Devil's own ink!" He pivoted toward a craftsman perched atop the mountain range. "Those clouds are all wrong! I want cumulus ice cream, and you're giving me cirrus cotton candy!"

"I hope you appreciate what you have in that man," I told my companions.

"Professionalism?" Joy suggested.

"Obsession," I said. "Without it, Hollywood wouldn't exist."

"Neither would the Empire of Japan," Yordan said. "Me, I'll take professionalism."

—

Our final stop of the day was a rambling brick structure with an adjoining Quonset hut, the whole installation bearing the code name *Château Mojave*. It was here that Joy and Admiral Yordan had arranged for me to meet my writer, my director, my costumers, and — most important of all — my reptilian alter ego. We entered the main building, a gloomy *atelier* permeated by the saccharine reek of glue and the smoky aroma of tanned leather. Artisans wearing New Amsterdam ID badges bustled about carrying dressmaker's dummies and rolls of fabric. Seated at the central worktable, two robust women — identical twins — sorted through a surreal inventory of eyeballs, talons, lizard scales, and webbed amphibian feet. Joy made the introductions. The creators of my behemoth suit were the celebrated Rubinstein sisters, Gladys and Mabel, who'd fashioned the full-scale, prophet-swallowing, profit-making whale for DeMille's *Voyage of Jonah*, as well as the gigantic crocodile for the same mogul's *Trials of Job*.

"We sewed the last stitch an hour ago," Gladys Rubinstein said, pointing toward the far corner. Cloaked in a tattered serape, a hulking mass rose against the window, blocking the daylight. "We'll do the unveiling when Brenda and Jimmy get here."

The talents to whom she referred, our temperamental writer and sardonic director, arrived only five minutes apart, each accompanied by a distressed ensign who looked like he'd rather be supervising a large African carnivore. These two Hollywood stalwarts were, respectively, the very Brenda Weisberg who'd goaded Darlene into writing *Corpuscula*, and the very James Whale who'd given the world the first two Frankenstein films. Within the monster-movie subculture of mid-forties Hollywood, Brenda was perceived as the sort of commendable hack without whom the industry couldn't function, but Whale was something else, a cult figure, an ambulatory myth. He dressed the part as well, his three-piece silk suit accessorized by an ascot and a walking stick.

"What are you working on now, Mr. Whale?" I asked, realizing too late that my question might be in bad taste.

"Beating the Japanese, Syms, just like you," he replied. "Call me Jimmy." His precise British accent struck me as cultivated in both senses of the word, as if he'd made the Shavian move of promoting himself to the upper class through sheer linguistic facility.

"I'm *thrilled* to be collaborating with you, Mr. Whale. Jimmy."

"Collaborating?" Whale echoed with amiable indignation. "Good heavens, Syms, you make us sound like a couple of Vichy quislings. By the way, I rarely patronize the cinema these days, so please don't ask me if I've seen your work. I'm sure it's marvelous. Truth to tell, I wanted Boris for the role, but apparently Dr. Groelish and his daughter wouldn't hear of anyone but the Monogram Shambler."

"Karloff is brilliant, but not quite athletic enough," Joy explained.

"May I assume Miss Weisberg brought the script with her?" Whale asked.

"She's not permitted to have that particular document on her person until we work out the kinks in her security clearance," Yordan said.

"I'm not sure I follow you," Whale said. "Are you saying Miss Weisberg was allowed to *write* the script, but she's not allowed to *possess* it?"

"She's not even allowed to *read* it," Yordan said. "So far, the only people who enjoy that privilege are Admiral Strickland, Secretary of State Byrnes, and Secretary of War Stimson. The old man wired his approval to China Lake this morning."

"You want a summary?" Brenda offered.

"Please," Whale said.

"I call it *What Rough Beast*."

"I don't get it," Yordan said.

"Yeats," Brenda said.

"We're at war, Miss Weisberg," Yordan said. "Poetry sends the wrong message."

"If anybody changes the title, I'm walking," Whale said.

"Jimmy, you are a man of breeding," I said.

"Savoir-fairy," Whale said with a sly grin.

"I see what you mean."

"I'm not sure you do, Syms. Love is a many-gendered thing."

At this juncture Dr. Groelish ambled into the Château Mojave, just in time to hear Brenda offer her précis of *What Rough Beast*.

"We start with a totally dark stage. Nighttime in Shirazuka. As the moon rises, so does Gorgantis, lurching out of Toyama

Bay like a monster from an aquatic hell."

"Gorgantis?" Whale said. "Tsk, tsk, that will never do."

"I like it," Joy said.

"You got a better idea, Jimmy?" Brenda asked.

"We're keeping it, Whale," Yordan said.

"The first engagement takes place entirely by moonlight," Brenda said. "The monster sinks every warship in the harbor, including the dreadnought *Yamato*, then wades ashore and devours an entire passenger train. End of act one."

"Does the *Yamato* defend herself?" Whale asked.

"O'Brien put working turrets on the foredeck," Yordan replied. "It fires BB's. Very impressive."

"After the sun comes up, Gorgantis tromps through the heart of the city, crushing and burning everything in his path," Brenda said. "The Japs send in what's left of the Imperial Air Force, but the monster swats the planes out of the sky like mosquitoes. End of act two."

"More of O'Brien's models?" Whale asked.

"Radio-controlled fighters and dive bombers," Yordan said, nodding.

"Finally, the lizard heads for the Chiaki Mountains, determined to bring the war to the Emperor's doorstep," Brenda said. "The enemy counterattacks with tanks and artillery, but Gorgantis melts them with his blazing breath. The climax comes when he leans over Mount Onibaba and pulps the Imperial Palace with his claws. Fade-out."

"Elapsed time?" Whale asked.

"Twenty-five minutes, a half-hour at most," Brenda said.

"Sounds about right," Yordan said. "We mustn't bore the delegation."

"I don't suppose I have any lines," I said.

"Only roars," Brenda said.

Yordan managed a glower with his good eye. "It's time you met your PRR."

Gladys seized the serape with both hands, whipping it away as abruptly as a magician unclothing a dinner table without disturbing the place settings. *Qui n'a plus qu'un moment a vivre n'a plus rien a dissimuler*, so let me now confess that the instant I laid eyes on my Personal Reptile Rig, I fell madly in love with it. To view a dwarf behemoth in a 16mm black-and-white longshot was one thing, to contemplate such a creature in the flesh quite another. Jaws dropping, eyes expanding, the *What Rough Beast* troupe stood in amazement before the Rubinsteins' creation, savoring the elegant green asbestos scales, golden dorsal plates, mighty tail, helical horns, swirling barbels, and tusks as bright and sharp as samurai swords.

"I can work with this," Whale said.

"Magnificent," Joy said.

"Spectacular," Dr. Groelish said.

"Fabulous," Brenda said.

"There's a backup suit in the Quonset hut," Mabel noted, "just in case this one gets damaged in the run-through."

"The Navy has always appreciated the power of redundancy," Yordan said.

"Syms, I have one word for you," Whale said. "Caliban."

"Of course," I said, as if I understood what he was getting at.

Although I could see no obvious connection between the son of Sycorax and my Gorgantis character, Whale obviously did, which probably explained why he was a living legend and I was starring in *Revenge of Corpuscula*.

"This is not a cerebral part," Whale elaborated. "You are a monster from the id. You are Death with haunches, *la Grande Faucheuse* with scales. Feel your way into your swampiest self. Cavort, gambol, improvise, surprise. 'Thou poisonous slave, got by the Devil himself upon thy wicked dam, come forth!'"

"Like hell he's going to improvise," Yordan said. "He's going to follow the script exactly."

"It's okay, Admiral," Brenda said. "I'm used to it. If I don't give the director material he can capriciously throw away on the set, I'm not doing my job."

Humming and cooing, the Rubinsteins began the laborious process of inserting me into their handiwork, which was really a kind of diving bell, its portals sealed with waterproof zippers, its air enriched with pure oxygen delivered by an aluminum cylinder embedded in the monster's stomach. Throughout the costuming procedure Whale entertained everyone with stories from what were for him, alas, already the good old days. The director was in mourning for the thirties, that freewheeling era when you could make a witty horror satire like *Bride of Frankenstein*, a slapstick sci-fi lark like *The Invisible Man*, or a fever dream like *The Old Dark House* without the front office fussing too much about whether the audience would get it. You could even shoot, for the original *Frankenstein*, Colin Clive delivering a deliciously blasphemous line after successfully vivifying his monster, and of course the censors would lift it from the soundtrack, leaving the actor's lips moving mutely on the screen, but how wonderful to realize he was saying, "Now I know what it's like to be God!"

Within a half-hour I was suited up. I felt simultaneously empowered and entombed. The PRR required me to endure many physical discomforts: the rubbery stench, the claustrophobic atmosphere, the torrid temperature, and, most of all, the pressure of Gorgantis's immense head, suspended several inches above my cranium on U-shaped braces clamped to my shoulders and separated from the creature's body by a neoprene seal — the idea being that if any water leaked into the mouth, the main cavity would remain dry. The skull and its contents weighed almost as much as the rest of the costume, being crammed not only with palisades of teeth but also the flamethrower nozzle, my Klaxon voice-box, and the batteries that illuminated the monster's eyes. Equally distressing was my limited field of vision, circumscribed by the tiny isinglass peepholes in my chest, which Gladys and Mabel had ingeniously wired to the eyeball batteries, lest my breath fog them up. Beyond these anomalies, the thing functioned essentially as a suit of clothes, with Gorgantis's ponderous hind legs encasing my equivalent limbs like a pair of seven-league boots, while my arms fit snugly into his forelegs and their attached claws. On Gladys's orders I wrapped my right hand around a squeezable bulb that through compressed-air technology would simultaneously open Gorgantis's jaws, activate his roar, and cause his tail to oscillate like a broom. Mabel, meanwhile, instructed me to curl my left hand around a similar bulb that, once my tail was filled with gasoline, would make smoke gush from my nostrils like steam from a tea kettle and flames leap from my mouth in great crimson streamers.

"You look terrific," Joy said.

Gingerly I attempted my first step. The walls of my rubbery crypt echoed with the coarse rhythm of my breathing. Despite my fears, the bulky suit came with me, tail and all, and I stayed on my feet. A second step. So far, so good. A third step. Miraculously, I didn't topple over.

My colleagues broke into spontaneous applause, with Whale remarking, in all seriousness, "This is going to be my comeback."

I tried a dozen more steps, getting halfway across the *atelier*, but then the great mass of the PRR — my epic thighs, titanic tail, the cylinder in my belly — began exacting its toll, and I paused to catch my breath.

"How're you doing?" Gladys asked.

"I wish you'd used lighter materials," I said, gasping, each word muffled by my vulcanized habitat.

"If you think it's heavy now, wait till they load your tail with petrol," Whale said.

"I'm having trouble keeping my balance," I said. "Will the gasoline stabilize me?"

"Probably not," Mabel said.

"So what should I do?"

"Practice, practice, practice," Whale said.

"Give us a roar, Syms," Joy said.

I squeezed my right hand, and there emerged from the be-hemoth's larynx a sound like nothing I'd ever heard before, a primordial, elemental, preternatural GRRAAGGHHH!, even as my tail swept the floor, sending chairs and wastebaskets hurtling in all directions. For one glowing moment Operation Fortune Cookie made complete sense to me. For a brief incandescent interval I believed that *What Rough Beast* was going to end the Pacific War. Now I knew what it was like to be God.

III

TIFFANY THE HOOKER left my room over an hour ago, off on another house call, but her apple face still floats through my mind, her lilting voice rings in my ear, and her wretched perfume lingers everywhere. Our intercourse, I should hasten to report, was entirely of the verbal variety, so if you're looking for something spicier than banter about Japanese monster movies, skip to the kinky encounter between Darlene and me that I'm planning to include later in this chapter. But for now I feel bound to say a few words about Tiffany's visit. Should I decide to cancel my jump, this tart with a heart of gold — evidently such creatures exist, which may be why my father never proscribed their appearance in movies — will deserve much of the credit.

I'd just finished writing about the Knickerbocker behemoths enjoying their quick little picnic at the bottom of China Lake, when someone started pounding on my door. The intruder proved to be a young woman costumed like a belly dancer, with baggy blue trousers, silver breastplates, and a sequined monkey jacket.

"Trick or treat!" she said.

I'd forgotten it was the weekend before Halloween. "Are you with the convention?"

"Nope, I'm Tiffany with the Starlight Escort Service," she said, holding up a Gladstone bag. "What convention?"

"Wonderama. Every monster-movie fan east of the Mississippi is here."

"That would explain the giant Gorgantis balloon on the roof. If you're Marty Kreske, allow me to escort you anywhere you want to go, from the hottest dance club to the deepest reaches of my gravy boat."

"Did you write that line yourself?"

"I wish. My big sister's in charge of the scripts. Lucy's got a knack for words. I use my tongue otherwise."

"I'm not Marty Kreske."

"Really? How come? It says Room 2014 right there on your door."

"True enough, but my name's Syms Thorley."

In pursuing our conversation, Tiffany and I soon decided that her intended customer was most likely staying in the hotel but that the Starlight dispatcher had transposed two digits when taking down the gentleman's room number. I invited Tiffany to use my phone. She called the desk and asked to be connected to Marty Kreske.

"The horny little sucker's supposed to be in 2014," she said demurely.

The mystery was soon solved. There was indeed a Kreske on the premises, and he had indeed ordered the Seraglio Special, three hundred dollars for two hours of Tiffany's parted thighs and undivided attention. However, he was just as glad that the dispatcher had turned 2041 into 2014, because he'd recently lost his wallet, probably through carelessness, possibly theft, and the consequent distress had doused his desire for an ersatz Turkish courtesan.

I was not surprised when, after thanking me for the phone, accepting a glass of amontillado, declining a cigarette, and heading for the door, Tiffany paused at the threshold and said, "I don't suppose..."

"You see before you a man who is suicidally depressed," I told her. "I'm not morally opposed to doing business with you, but I wouldn't be able to hold up my end of things."

"What've you got to be suicidally depressed about?" she asked, drifting back into the room.

"Something I did before you were born. Or didn't do. This morning, for some reason, it all came home to roost."

"You want to talk about it?"

"No."

"If I gave you a blowjob, maybe that would change your point of view."

"You're sweet."

"No, I'm out three hundred dollars."

"I'm sorry."

"It's happened before."

"I should get back to work."

For Tiffany a passable paraphrase of "I should get back to work" was evidently "Please make yourself at home," because now she sauntered toward my desk, seized my Raydo, and, settling onto the green Naugahyde ottoman, scrutinized the statuette with a combination of perplexity and wonderment. "*Syms K. Thorley, Lifetime Achievement Award, Balti-more Imagi-Movies Society, 1984,*" she read. "Are you a movie director?"

"An actor."

"Really? Me, too, in a way, only except they don't give out trophies on my side of the street. Have I seen any of your pictures?"

"Tiffany, darling, there's over fifty dollars in my wallet. It's all yours. Where I'm going they don't accept cash, just indulgences, and then only if you're Catholic."

"Why is the monster attacking a lighthouse?" she asked, caressing the pewter rhedosaurus.

"The original story is about a lighthouse keeper who discovers that, once a year, a lonely sea-dwelling dinosaur answers the call of his foghorn."

"The dinosaur wants a friend?"

"A friend, yes. But he's the last of his kind."

"That's so sad."

"The idea got lost in the transition to the screen. Ray Bradbury called his story 'The Fog Horn.' The movie ended up as *The Beast from 20,000 Fathoms*."

"That's a better title." Tiffany set the Raydo back atop my manuscript, thus resurrecting its function as a paperweight. "The easiest way to kill yourself, I've heard, is to tie a plastic bag around your head. That's my plan if I ever get cancer."

"I'm thinking of leaping out the window," I said, retrieving my wallet from atop the television.

"I can't accept your money without giving you something in return."

"Consider it a retainer against a future blowjob."

"Kind of a down payment?" Tiffany said, her voice rising so I wouldn't miss the joke.

I slid all fifty-three dollars from my wallet, and, taking her creamy hand, each finger adorned with silver rings and hot-pink nail polish, pressed the bills into her palm. Come morning, of course, I would need money to tip the shuttle driver and grab some coffee at the airport, but I could always cash a check at the desk on my way out.

"I go to the movies a lot," Tiffany said. "I've probably seen you on the big screen without knowing it."

"Only if you're a Gorgantis fan."

"Gorgantis? The same Gorgantis they've got on the roof?" She extended her arm, fluttering her decorous fingers. "You're shitting me! You're a Gorgantis actor? I *love* those movies! My favorite is *Gorgantis Strikes Back*. Were you in that one?"

"I'm afraid so."

"What about *Fury of Mechagorgantis*?" she asked, popping the money into her Gladstone bag.

"I was in that one, too."

"How did they make you look so Japanese?"

"You're correct to suppose I needed a lot of makeup — but not so I'd look Japanese."

"Huh?"

"Think about it."

Tiffany lit up like a jack-o'-lantern. "Hey, wow, *now* I understand! This is so cool! I can't believe I'm standing here talking to Gorgantis himself! I wish I had a video for you to autograph."

Driven by my natural Darwinian instinct for self-promotion, I told Tiffany she could acquire such merchandise in the Wonderama huckster's room on the mezzanine level, but she'd have to act quickly, because it closed in twenty minutes. She spun around and fled my suite. I went back to work, narrating the rest of the briefing bunker scene, Admiral Strickland's reluctant revelation that President Truman had endorsed the China Lake Petition. A half-hour later Tiffany returned, bearing not only a VHS cassette of *Gorgantis vs. Miasmica* but an indelible magic marker. I signed the slipcase using my most florid pseudo-calligraphy.

"And now, if you'll excuse me, I'm trying to beat a deadline," I said, an assertion that, transmogrified by Tiffany's imagination, became a request that she insert the movie in the VCR and start watching it while sprawled across my bed.

I resumed my autobiographical efforts, recounting my conversation with Obie as I stood in Hangar A admiring his Shirazuka model. Tiffany thoughtfully kept the soundtrack of *Gorgantis vs. Miasmica* as low as possible. We took turns hitting the amontillado and the Camel filters. At one point my roommate picked up the phone and, without consulting me, ordered dinner for both of us. Somehow she intuited that I was fond of chicken cacciatore, even the kind they serve in Holiday Inns.

After the food arrived, we lay on the bed together watching the rest of *Gorgantis vs. Miasmica*. The picture was better than I remembered. My performance struck me as flamboyant without being overwrought. I'd forgotten how skillfully

I did the ju-jitsu moves. Throughout the second-act climax, which involved the monsters trying to stuff each other down an active volcano, Tiffany emitted noises that I chose to interpret as gasps of excitement, though perhaps she was suppressing a laugh.

I finished my chicken and returned to my labors, writing about the unveiling of my PRR in the Château Mojave. Shortly after setting down Jimmy Whale's line, "Practice, practice, practice," I glanced toward the bed. Tiffany was gone. A piece of Holiday Inn stationery lay on the pillow. She'd written her message with the same indelible marker I'd used to sign the video.

> *Dear Mr. Thorley,*
>
>   *Thanks to you, this was the best Halloween weekend ever. I really enjoyed* Gorgantis vs. Miasmica, *especially knowing it was you fighting the walking toxic waste dump.*
>
>   *Whatever you did before I was born, even if it was murdering somebody, jumping out a window won't fix it.*
>
>   *I believe that one day the dinosaur will find another of his kind, instead of just a lighthouse.*
>
>   *Your friend,*
>   *Tiffany Nolan*

The amontillado is nearly depleted, but I've still got plenty of ink and paper. The cigs are holding out, too. If all goes well, by midnight I'll have finished describing our chaotic *What Rough Beast* rehearsal. Farewell, my adorable Tiffany. I'll always be a little bit in love with you.

Practice, practice, practice, Jimmy Whale had said, but Admiral Yordan still detested the idea of my taking the Gorgantis suit home with me, and he remained unsympathetic even after Gladys and Mabel reminded him about the backup PRR in the Quonset hut. For the next hour Whale tried to convince Yordan that I could never deliver a transcendent performance unless I spent as much time as possible inhabiting the behemoth's neoprene flesh.

"I don't really expect you to understand, Admiral, but this is about *art*," Whale said. "It's about the ineffable, the irreducible, the *Je ne sais quoi*."

"I've heard quite enough French from you today, Whale," Yordan said.

"A convincing performance is always rooted in the body," Whale said. "The suit must become Thorley's second skin. Stanislavski discoursed eloquently on this principle."

"The next time I want to read a Communist queer, Stanislavski will be my first choice," Yordan told Whale. "Unless, of course, you've written on the subject yourself."

"If you're worried about somebody spotting the PRR, let me point out that the costume is its own camouflage," Dr. Groelish noted. "Our boy here could put on his lizard rig and saunter down Wilshire Boulevard in broad daylight, and who would ever imagine the thing was designed to spook the Japanese?"

"I still think it should stay here," Yordan said.

"Let's take it from the top," Whale said. "If Syms doesn't become one with the lizard, the game is over."

As twilight seeped across the Mojave Desert, Yordan at long last threw up his hands and grunted in resignation. With co-lossal reluctance he got on the phone and arranged delivery of a Navy panel truck to the *atelier*, anything with "a cargo bay large enough to accommodate a half-dozen oxygen cylin-ders and a dwarf behemoth." While the admiral talked to the captain of the motor pool, Mabel explained that she wouldn't be fueling my tail until the day of the run-through. She didn't want me fooling around with Gorgantis's incendiary capabili-ties before I'd had a formal lesson in flamethrowing. Mean-while I should concentrate on walking backward, going grace-fully downstairs, and climbing out of private swimming pools with balletic poise.

When the panel truck arrived, Yordan slapped a Class T gas-rationing sticker on the windshield, thereby entitling me to unlimited fill-ups, just like a senator, plus a coupon book good for a walloping two hundred gallons. He further equipped me with a two-way wrist radio of the sort worn by Ralph Byrd in Republic's Dick Tracy serials. This one was not a prop, Yordan explained. Between now and the great rehearsal, I must contact Commander Quimby every morning at pre-cisely 0900 hours — the transceiver was preset to Quimby's identical device — then again at noon, with subsequent calls at

1500 hours and 1800 hours, no exceptions, rain or shine, fair or foul, hell or high water.

Shortly after midnight, my flesh throbbing with exhaustion, my head spinning with the doctrine of reptilian intimidation, I reached Santa Monica and pulled into my garage: as safe a place as any to store the PRR, I figured. I made my weary way to the bungalow. Darlene sat at the kitchen table, smoking a cigarette and drawing x's through certain presumably gratuitous speeches in my *Lycanthropus* script. My favorite lines, no doubt, but that didn't mean they deserved to stay. For the next hour I mesmerized her with my adventures at China Lake, repeatedly stating my sincere opinion that she would have given my employers a script far better than Brenda's formulaic Armageddon. Much to Darlene's delight, I packed a large quantity of treason into the presentation, until eventually I had no more top secrets to reveal, only perfunctory and jejune secrets, so I ended my unlikely narrative and asked her what she thought of Operation Fortune Cookie.

"To use a line I promised myself I would never write," she said, "'It's just crazy enough to work.'"

"If they were planning to overhaul the script, I would've brought your name up, but the whole thing's set in stone."

"It's okay," Darlene said. "I'm not jealous." She took a drag on her Chesterfield. "So do you think there's going to be a sequel?"

Eight hours later I reported for duty at Monogram. As the morning's labors progressed, I found myself appreciating the

Navy's wisdom in declining to draft me but instead allowing *Revenge of Corpuscula* to go forward as planned. Neither Beaudine, Katzman, Dagover, nor Dudley the AD bothered to ask what I'd done during my mysterious Tuesday sojourn in the desert. As long as we delivered our program to the exhibitors on schedule, my trips to China Lake would evidently arouse no untoward curiosity at Monogram or any other redoubt of the home front.

While I was gone Trixie had secured the necessary orangutan costume. It turned out that Republic was shooting a jungle adventure down the street, and they were willing to lease the suit for only a hundred bucks. Beaudine's brother-in-law showed up drunk, which I suspect made his performance all the more convincingly simian. Like the patriotic iguana I was, I called Commander Quimby on my Dick Tracy set at nine o'clock, then again at noon, assuring him that Gorgantis and I were both in good condition.

The afternoon's shoot proved grueling, the toughest yet on a Corpuscula picture, but by seven-thirty we'd managed to get six pages in the can: scene 18, the alchemical creature convincing Dr. Niemuller to turn Bongowi into a meat-eater, and scene 19, the carnivorous ape's subsequent assault on Dr. Werdistratus. Later that night, after our usual spaghetti dinner followed by a productive two-hour session that found Darlene and me polishing my *Lycanthropus* screenplay into a shining B-movie gem, I decided to do my Gorgantis homework, so we hauled the rig out of the truck and dragged it into the parlor. Darlene couldn't get over the sheer demented brilliance of the thing. She called it "uncanny," "haunting," and — she intended this as praise — "perverse." As she stood behind me on a step-ladder, cradling the great head against her chest, I inserted my feet in the soft vulcanized leggings and my hands in the neoprene claws. After activating the glowing eyeballs, Darlene descended to ground level, seized the pull-tab above my tail, and climbed the ladder again, thus bringing the teeth of the dorsal zipper into alignment. So there I was, encased once again in my scales and talons, a Cretaceous visitation bent on teaching Admiral Nagumo how right he'd been to imagine that his attack on Pearl Harbor had awakened a sleeping dragon.

"I can't speak for my entire gender," Darlene said, "but I think he's the sexiest monster ever to hit Hollywood."

Grasping the knob in my navel, I gave it a quarter turn, and an instant later came the soothing, serpentine hiss of pure oxygen seeping into my suit. "I'm supposed to start out with a few simple exercises. Walking backward, standing on one leg, stuff like that."

"No, darling. I need something more from you tonight."

"Huh?"

"My glands are pumping, Syms. We're going down to the beach."

"I don't understand."

"Men. It's a Fay Wray thing. Every girl wants a big snorting schlemiel she can wrap around her little finger. We'll start out with business as usual, Gorgantis kidnapping his leading lady, but eventually she'll conquer him through sheer nerve and spunkiness."

When Darlene got like this there was no sense in resisting, so I waited patiently while she changed into her bathing suit, after which we loaded the lizard rig, Syms Thorley still inside, into the Navy truck and took off, Darlene driving almost as recklessly as Joy Groelish, or so I inferred from all the rocking and swaying to which the PRR and I were subjected. At last the vibrations stopped. Next came the clanking and clanging of Darlene opening the cargo bay doors. I insisted on shambling out by myself. Practice, practice, practice.

Aided by the full moon, my luminous eyeballs, and Darlene's hand, I wended my way through the undulating palms of Palisades Park, eventually reaching a broad swath of sand. I lumbered south, the Pacific breakers to my right, Darlene on my left, my tail growing heavier by the minute. Arriving at the Municipal Pier, we took refuge in a dank forest of pilings. We glanced in all directions. The literal coast was literally clear. At two o'clock in the morning, everybody in Santa Monica evidently had better things to do with his time than wandering around on a desolate beach that stank of rotting kelp.

"Carry me into the water," Darlene demanded.

"Why?"

"It's romantic."

I picked her up and, hooking one scaly arm under her knees while looping the other around her shoulders, began the requested abduction. It was a familiar gesture for me. Kha-Ton-Ra usually made off with the heroine in this fashion at least once per picture, and occasionally the same impulse overcame Corpuscula. But I'd never done it as Gorgantis before, and never with Darlene. Soon I hit the tide line, an undulating ribbon of pebbles and seaweed, then kept on going, wading into the surf — for such was my co-star's desire — heading in the general direction of Hawaii. The bay rose gently, climbing to my knees, my thighs, my bulbous abdomen. Inside the suit, all was well — Gladys and Mabel had successfully waterproofed the rig — more than well, thanks to the oxygen cylinder: temperate, balmy, sublime.

"No, Gorgantis!" Darlene cried. "You are a sea creature, but I am of the land! Take me back to the shore!"

I squeezed my roar-bulb. *"Grraagghhh!"*

"Take me back now!"

Pivoting, I started for the beach.

"Gorgantis, set me down!"

The behemoth obeyed.

"This way," she said, clasping my claw and leading me toward the pier.

"Grraagghhh!"

No sooner had we entered our grotto beneath the boardwalk than my amazing lover, this lissome woman whose urges were now at the boiling point, gave free rein to her imagination. She grabbed my dorsal zipper, pulling the slide downward inch by inch until she'd created an aperture large enough to admit her slender form. Having opened me up, she now proceeded to enter me, first slithering around my spine, then planting her willowy thighs and calves next to mine in the monster's leggings. A remarkable performance, but it wasn't over yet. As we stood face to face, our bodies clamped pleasurably together, she seized the interior tab and closed the breach, sealing us within the lizard like unborn twins navigating their mother's womb. This scenario was not entirely unfamiliar to us. Two years earlier we'd seen an unbowdlerized cut of Sam Wood's *For Whom the Bell Tolls* at Grauman's Chinese Theatre, right before the censors snipped out the famous sleeping bag tryst between Robert Jordan and Maria.

"Where do the noses go?" Darlene asked, retrieving a foil-wrapped prophylactic from the bodice of her swimming suit. I'd never heard her do Ingrid Bergman before. It was a flawless impersonation.

"Maria," I said, Gary Cooper's uninformative response.

Several minutes later, I died. 'Twas beauty killed the beast. Practice, practice, practice.

The next day's *Revenge of Corpuscula* shoot found me tackling a relatively simple scene: the monster's big courtroom speech, in which he explains to the magistrate and the burgomaster that they have no right to put him on trial, "for I am merely an external manifestation of the ghastliness within your own souls." I didn't understand that line, and neither did anybody else, including Darlene, who wrote it, but my delivery nevertheless pleased Beaudine, as did the rest of my performance, and the shoot ended earlier than expected. Not long after Dudley declared that we were finished for the day, a gawky Navy courier appeared bearing the final draft of *What Rough Beast*. He explained that I must read the script right now, furtively and silently, whereupon he would spirit it back to China

Lake. He called me "sir." I liked that. We retired to my dressing room. Every page was stamped TOP SECRET, but beyond that anomaly I found few deviations from Brenda's Tuesday presentation. The only conspicuous addition was Admiral Yordan's opening monologue, an exhortation to the effect that the behemoths were an unprecedented weapon against which ordinary heroism would prove pointless.

Over the next four shooting days, thanks to Beaudine's efficiency and Katzman's tyranny, we managed to finish every set-up except one — the monster's long monologue when he awakes with the supercerebrum in his skull — which Dudley had scheduled for Thursday, but then I explained that, alas, I would be gone that afternoon, working on my secret military assignment, and if Dudley didn't like it, he should go talk to Katzman. When not declaiming Darlene's dialogue on stage three, reporting to Commander Quimby on my Dick Tracy set, and studiously observing the movements of terrestrial lizards at a Route 101 roadside attraction called Clem and Bertha's Reptile World, I subjected myself to seven more rounds of Gorgantis calisthenics, four solo, three involving my girlfriend and her Fay Wray fantasy. In consequence of this demanding regimen, I lost seventeen pounds. Among the many non-fiction books I'll never get around to writing is *The Giant Mutant Fire-Breathing Bipedal Iguana Diet*.

On Thursday morning, shortly after 1100 hours, I arrived at China Lake for the run-through. My first stop was the Château Mojave, where, per the contract, Joy and Dr. Groelish presented me with half my salary: a $5,000 check issued by the

United States Treasury and signed by Henry Morgenthau himself. While Gladys placed a fresh oxygen cylinder in Gorgantis's stomach, Mabel filled his tail with gasoline from red aluminum cans. As a joke, I gave her a five-gallon coupon from my ration book, which she immediately slipped into her purse.

After helping me into the PRR, the twins led me outside, then pointed toward three pyramids of orange crates intended to represent O'Brien's models of Shirazuka's buildings and landmarks. Languidly I lumbered onto the shooting range, unhappy to be dragging an extra thirty pounds of fossil fuel behind me. Suddenly Jimmy Whale appeared, pacing fretfully among the fragile targets, aglow in his white linen suit like a statue carved from phosphorus.

"What's the magic word?" he asked.

"Caliban," I said.

"'This thing of darkness I acknowledge mine,'" Whale said.

"There's a one-way valve in the nozzle," Gladys told the director. "Right now the regulator's in position five, wide open."

"Ready to breathe fire, Syms?" Whale asked.

"It's every actor's secret wish," I said.

"Just squeeze the burn-bulb," Gladys told me. "Slowly but steadily."

I did as instructed, and a thick jet of flame spewed from the behemoth's mouth. The blast struck the first pyramid head-on, instantly reducing it to ash.

"Much too quick," Whale said. "Stop it down all the way."

Mabel reached into Gorgantis's maw and set the regulator to position one.

"Open fire, Caliban," Whale said.

An incisive ribbon of burning gasoline shot forth, bisecting the second pyramid with the precision of a welder's torch cutting sheet metal. The whole configuration collapsed, but none of the crates caught fire.

"Impressive, but not apocalyptic," Whale said.

Next we tried position three, which gave us a growling shaft of flame that transmuted the third pyramid into a vivid, riveting, altogether satisfying conflagration.

"This porridge is just right," Whale said.

"*Mazel tov*," Mabel said.

"On with the show," Gladys said.

We ate lunch in the Château Mojave, feasting on a surprisingly tasty mulligan stew that Whale had improvised from available ingredients. Just as Gladys and Mabel finished zipping me into the PRR again, a troop transport vehicle appeared in the sandy parking lot, Admiral Yordan's personal chauffeur behind the wheel. I shambled up the ramp to the canopied load bed without assistance — practice, practice, practice — and then we took off, Whale and the Rubinstein twins following in the director's battered Rolls Royce, Joy and Dr. Groelish bringing up the rear in her convertible.

The ethos of a demented circus held dominion in Hangar B, a whirling hurly-burly that put me in mind of the traveling carnival that opened Robert Florey's artsy little Poe adaptation of '32, *Murders in the Rue Morgue*. Sailors bustled about, relaying messages, delivering coffee, and installing fire extinguishers at each corner of the model metropolis. Stagehands winched aloft the gigantic glass moon that would illuminate the sea battle. While a score of Obie's artisans put the finishing touches on the facsimile of the facsimile of the hypothetical city, a squad of Seabees channeled a thousand gallons of fresh water into Toyama Bay from a storage tank on the roof. Naval officers paced the perimeter of ill-starred Shirazuka, trying without success to look essential to the operation.

My entrance as Gorgantis caused an understandable stir. Except for Admiral Yordan, nobody in Hangar B had seen the lizard rig before. But an instant later, duty called — American boys were fighting and dying in the Pacific — and everybody went back to work.

Had I not already beheld the miniature in Hangar A, I might have assumed that Shirazuka's present incarnation was intended for the eyes of the Japanese delegation. While lacking the exquisite details of the final model, it was hardly the shoddy affair Joy had led me to expect. If the rehearsal went badly, it would not be for lack of a proper set.

Equipped now with a bullhorn, Whale placed an avuncular hand on my shoulder. "Remember, Caliban, you must seek your soul's darkest sanctum. Get thee to Sycorax's foulest fen and revel in the muck."

"Just so he sticks to the script," Yordan said, arriving in our vicinity.

"I am not familiar with your credentials as a director," Whale said.

"I don't have any — but then again, you're not a Naval officer," Yordan said.

"I've seen more of war's horrors than you," Whale said.

And with that my director kissed me on the snout, traded scowls with Yordan, and climbed the ladder of a lifeguard stand that the Navy had evidently commandeered from the private sector — the sign on the tower read *Redondo Beach Aquatic Club*. Whale didn't need to call for quiet on the set. The mere sight of this Hollywood god perched in his empyrean was enough to bring silence to Hangar B.

"Places, everyone!" Whale ordered.

The artisans abandoned their labors and melted into the shadows. Stagehands scurried up the ladders to the catwalks and manned the klieg lights. Ordnance technicians assumed their positions before the master control console.

"Musicians!" Whale called from on high.

"Musicians?" Yordan shouted. "What the hell are you talking about?"

"I hired an orchestra," Whale explained.

"An orchestra? Why, for Christ's sake?"

"To play the score."

"Score?"

"Mr. Waxman wrote us a score."

"And how do you intend to *pay* your musicians?" Yordan asked.

"The Midget Lizard Initiative hasn't been officially shut down yet," Whale explained. "Dr. Groelish still has a large discretionary fund. Mr. Waxman agreed to write an overture, a main theme, and a dozen cues for only three thousand dollars, considerably less than what you're paying me."

A side door opened, and a parade of musicians filed silently into the hangar, forty or so men and women gripping violins, violas, cellos, trumpets, cornets, clarinets, flutes, and percussion instruments, led by a bronze-haired conductor in a tweed jacket. It was indeed Franz Waxman, who'd composed the music for *Bride of Frankenstein* and *Evil of Corpuscula*.

"Those people better all have security clearances!" Yordan screamed.

"Please calm down, Admiral," Whale said. "You're getting on my nerves."

Approaching a grid of folding chairs at the back of the hangar, the musicians assumed their seats and prepared to play the overture.

"Kliegs off!" Whale shouted.

The stagehands complied.

"House lights off!"

A sailor opened a box mounted on the far wall and began flicking switches, plunging the hangar into a lugubrious gloom. The only illumination came from the tiny bulbs brightening the Shirazuka houses, the public lighting along the city's streets, and the cowled lamps on the orchestra's music stands.

"Moon!"

The huge sphere glowed to life, its reflection sparkling softly in Toyama Bay.

"Gorgantis, find your mark!"

Gladys and Mabel took me by the claws and led me across the same threshold by which we'd entered the studio. Shuffling along the outside wall of the hangar, the Mojave sun wringing dollops of sweat from all my pores, I was tempted to grab my

navel and open the valve on my oxygen cylinder, but I knew it
would be best to conserve that precious resource. We reached
the stage door, passed through the jamb, and followed a corru-
gated aluminum tunnel to the dry hatch on the bathyscaphe.
As I dropped to my knees, Mabel turned the wheel-lock, then
pulled back the great circular slab. I wriggled inside the chamber. The ceiling was barely a yard high, and I had to lie prone
on my bulging belly like a fat soldier crawling under barbed
wire.

Gladys and Mabel jammed my tail into the tiny compartment, then stepped away, sealing the hatch behind them. I
was doubly entombed, a man inside a lizard inside a bronze
casket. My underwater habitat was evidently wired for sound,
because I had no trouble hearing Yordan's monologue and the
accompanying Japanese translation.

"Honorable emissaries, you are about to witness the de-
structive fury of the most terrible weapon yet placed in the
hands of man! There can be no valor in resisting such a force!
The warrior who would take the field against a behemoth will
reap nothing for his courage beyond a bereaved wife and fa-
therless children!"

Waxman began conducting his overture, a frenzied, dissonant composition in which exotic Oriental chords and conventional Western progressions fought for supremacy within
the listener's reeling brain.

"The doors of hell open!" Yordan cried. "The beast rises!
Doom comes to Shirazuka!"

The overture built to its frantic climax. I turned the wheel-lock on the wet hatch, yanking with all my reptilian strength. As the bay flooded the compartment, I forced my way through the opening, then assumed a crouch on the floor of the pool. The music faded. I rotated the valve in my navel. A stream of cool air flowed forth, soughing against my rubbery shell. Now came the majestic "Gorgantis Theme," as we would eventually call it. I straightened my knees. With ponderous malevolence the behemoth breached Toyama Bay, then threw back his head, roared above the stately melody, and made ready to sack the city.

Although we got through the entire script in a mere three hours, with a satisfyingly flattened Shirazuka to show for our efforts, the run-through was a mélange of misadventures. When Whale ordered the dreadnought *Yamato* and her sister warships to shell the monster, her guns emitted not BB's but only feeble puffs of smoke. The passenger train I was supposed to devour hurtled off its trestle before I could seize it. As I set about trampling a factory complex underfoot, the counterattacking fighter planes and dive bombers lost their bearings, some crashing into Mount Onibaba, others suffering fatal encounters with the lifeguard stand, only a few getting close enough for me to bat them out of the air as the script required. And while Gladys had carefully set the flamethrower nozzle to position three, the regulator had evidently gone kablooey during the bumpy journey to Hangar B, because the gasoline streamed forth with uncontrolled exuberance, so that much of Shirazuka was instantly immolated in an exhibition as per-

functory as a fireworks display at a church picnic. Disappointment clouded the sailors' faces as they smothered the residual
flames.

Surprisingly, none of these disasters fazed Whale. He
declined to chew out Obie over the obstreperous props or
scold the Rubinstein twins for acquiring a persnickety flamethrower. *Au contraire*, the worse things went, the more fun
Whale seemed to be having. Perhaps he subscribed to the
principle that a disastrous dress rehearsal portends a successful opening night — a truism that in my experience happens
to be true. Instead of indulging in a Katzmanian tirade or a
Beaudinesque sulk, this suave gentleman put all his energies
into his art, feeding me brilliant bit after brilliant bit as I performed my slow dance on the killing ground. When we prac-
ticed the sea battle, Whale suggested that I seize two aircraft
carriers and smack their flight decks together to the crash of
cymbals, a sound that Waxman's percussionist was pleased to
provide. Under the master's direction the behemoth's appetite
for human flesh became a darkly comic affair, with Gorgantis
stuffing Nipponese homunculi into his mouth like handfuls of
popcorn. After the Japanese armored divisions took up their
positions in the Chiaki Mountains, prepared to defend the
Emperor at any cost, Whale had me grab the Chi-Ro tanks two
at a time, soften them with my breath, and tie their gun barrels together, the resulting configurations suggesting knotted
pairs of socks.

Only once that afternoon did Whale waft out a genuinely
bad idea. Calling down from his lofty roost, he asked Obie

whether Gorgantis might gouge and scrape Mount Onibaba with his claws until it became a bust of Hirohito, which the monster would then pulverize. Before Obie could reply, a chorus of suppressed groans arose. Absorbing this spontaneous critique, the director declared that on second thought it would be better simply to plant a large packet of stage blood in the Imperial Palace.

Whale's greatest contribution to *What Rough Beast* was a concept that lay outside the domain of Brenda's script. How poignant it would be, he decided, if our visiting emissaries found themselves hoping against hope that the dwarf behemoth might, just might, perish before completing his mission. Thus, when the attack reached its inevitable climax, with Shirazuka smoldering and Gorgantis triumphant, the delegation's shock would be that much greater. And so it was that Whale had me lurch back in feigned agony when my claws sliced through a mass of high-tension power lines, and he coached me to appear exhausted — faint, almost — as I kicked downtown Shirazuka to pieces. Right before the final assault on the mountain, Whale stopped the rehearsal and ordered the ordnance technicians to supplement the BB's in the defenders' tanks with tiny blisters of red dye. When the battle resumed, the effect was exactly what Whale envisioned: a ripped, stricken, bullet-ridden Gorgantis, bleeding from a hundred wounds, but still charging toward the Imperial Palace, as if his unconquerable soul knew nothing of his torn flesh.

The klieg lights faded, ensconcing the victorious reptile in the shadows beyond the city. Slowly I shambled toward my director, receiving congratulatory strokes and pats along the way. Whale descended from the lifeguard stand. He thanked everyone for their work on "an auspiciously catastrophic rehearsal," then tenderly caressed my dorsal plates and said, "Caliban, my friend, we've got a hit on our hands."

"You're not a man in a suit," Joy told me. "You're a living, breathing mutant iguana."

"I'm going to nominate you for an Oscar," Gladys said.

"The *Yamato*'s guns will be working in time for the performance," Obie assured me. "The planes, too."

"And the flamethrower," Mabel said.

Now Yordan came swaggering onto the scene. Appropriating Whale's bullhorn, he informed the assembled artisans, technicians, and military men that he had heartening news from Washington.

"Yesterday Foreign Minister Togo cabled Secretary Byrnes and told him the composition of the delegation," Yordan said, flourishing a document. Glimpsing the paper through my isinglass peepholes, I saw that it was stamped TOP SECRET. "Obviously they're taking our demonstration shot seriously, because it's a darned impressive line-up." The admiral scanned the classified communiqué with his solitary eye. "Deputy Foreign Minister Toshikazu Kase, Chief Cabinet Secretary Hisatsune Sakomizu, Director of Information Hiroshi Shimomura, and — here's the kicker — Marquis Koichi Kido, Lord Keeper of the Privy Seal and principal aide and advisor to the Emperor."

Cheers and applause reverberated through the hangar.

"The show starts at 1500 hours sharp, Sunday, June 3, 1945, a date that will live in the annals of diplomacy," Yordan said. "Mr. O'Brien, your ordnance technicians must be in their places by 1400 hours. Mr. Thorley, I want to see you suiting up in the Château Mojave no later than 1100 hours."

"Get me out of this goddamn iguana," I said. "A man could suffocate in here."

Slowly, tentatively, with the shuffling gait of the zombie roustabouts in Monogram's *Voodoo Circus*, the exhausted cast and crew of *What Rough Beast* emerged from Hangar B into the glare of a brilliant sunset, its crimson rays spreading across the desert sky like lacerations wrought by reptilian talons. Here at the Naval Ordnance Test Station, rosy-fingered dawns were doubtless common, but so were bloody-clawed dusks.

Gladys and Mabel loaded the PRR into the cargo bay of the troop transport. Before I could assume the passenger seat, Joy squeezed my arm and said she would like my companionship while she performed "a painful but necessary duty over by the lake." I arranged for Yordan's chauffeur to drop the suit back at the Château Mojave, and then my liaison and I took off in her Chevy.

"They're all dead," she said abruptly.

"The citizens of Shirazuka?" I asked.

"The first generation of dwarfs — Rex, Evelyn, and Oswald. We lost them two days ago to Hutchinson-Gilford syndrome."

"Never heard of it."

"Progeria. Premature aging. Luckily, in April we hatched a second generation — Huey, Dewey, and Louie. They've got progeria, too, but they'll probably live three more weeks at least, long enough for us to exhibit them to the delegation."

Reaching the lake shore, we headed north through a tract of desert that, Joy informed me, concealed at least twenty species of lizard and almost as many sorts of snake. Every day, as the sun lifted toward its zenith, the creatures would crawl free of their dens to warm themselves on the omnipresent rocks.

"Believe me, it wasn't easy figuring out how to make the descendants of cold-blooded iguanas breathe fire," she said. "Once the Knickerbocker Project gets declassified, we'll publish a dozen papers in the *Journal of Evolutionary Biology*."

After a journey of three miles, my liaison pulled over, parked the car, and opened the trunk. Arrayed in purple blossoms, three potted hedgehog cacti sat in a cardboard box along with a red trowel and a pair of canvas work gloves. Together Joy and I bore the cacti toward the lake. Because Rex, Evelyn, and Oswald had loved to swim and dive, Joy had buried them within view of the water. Their graves were marked with crosses and protected by a natural ring of boulders.

"When the time comes, I'll help you eulogize Huey, Dewey, and Louie, too," I said.

"I'd appreciate that," Joy said.

Her voice now acquired a dreamy, otherworldly timbre. I thought of Gale Sondergaard's eerie performance as the medium in *Uncanny*, a serviceable supernatural thriller that Darlene once wrote for Katzman between Corpuscula pictures.

"Long ago in Japan, a young woman named Momoko hired

a fishing boat and rowed to the most far-flung of the Oki Islands, north of Honshu. She planned to rescue her father, a great warrior imprisoned by the Emperor, whose occasional fits of madness caused him to mistreat even his most devoted samurai. Sailing around the island, Momoko came upon a wrenching scene: a maiden robed in white, standing on a bluff. Her parents knelt beside her, weeping piteously. As Momoko put to shore, she spotted a priest, who explained that each year the locals sacrificed a maiden to the dragon Yofuné-Nushi, ruler of the deep and lord of tempests."

Availing herself of the trowel and gloves, Joy planted the largest cactus on Rex's grave.

"To the grieving parents' infinite gratitude, Momoko offered to take the maiden's place. She put on the ceremonial white kimono, clasped a warrior's dagger between her teeth, and leaped into the green depths. Down, down she plummeted, swimming with great skill, for as a child she'd dived with the pearl fishers of her village. Soon she reached the ocean floor, where she came upon a cavern. Venturing into the undersea grotto, Momoko found a sleeping dragon, his scales trailing tatters of his victims' robes, his serpentine body coiled around a curious treasure: a jade statue of the Emperor who had imprisoned her father."

Here Joy paused to root the second cactus above Evelyn's remains.

"Suddenly Yofuné-Nushi awoke and attacked the warrior-woman. They fought furiously, but the battle soon ended when Momoko drove her dagger through the dragon's right eye and straight into his brain. Calling upon all her remaining air and residual strength, she swam free of the grotto, the jade figurine pressed against her breast. No sooner had Momoko breached the surface than the monstrous corpse came bobbing up behind her. On the beach, the thankful maiden and her parents waited to shower Momoko with kisses."

Joy allowed me to install the third cactus, a tribute to Oswald, then continued her tale.

"Several days later, hearing that Yofuné-Nushi had been vanquished and his treasure recovered, the prince of the island sent word to the Emperor. The messengers returned bearing extraordinary news. Years ago an evil magician had cursed the jade statue and presented it to Yofuné-Nushi — but shortly after Momoko's victory, the Emperor's madness had mysteriously passed. When Momoko and her father returned to Honshu, the chastened monarch, horrified to realize he'd abused his faithful samurai, immediately freed him and arranged many honors for Momoko, slayer of dragons."

"I like that story," I said.

"Once this war is over, Syms, I'm going into veterinary medicine."

"Good idea."

"If Admiral Strickland approaches me with big plans for another strategic lizard, I'll kick him in the balls."

"I hope I'm there to see it."

"Veterinarians are my heroes. Do you have any heroes, Syms?"

"I once knew a herpetologist named Ivan Groelish who

tried to end the Second World War through the craziest damn scheme you ever heard. The odds were against him, but his heart was in the right place."

IV

MIDNIGHT HAS COME to Edgar Allan Poe's city. Luckily, I remembered to place an order with room service just before the kitchen shut down for the day. The present writing session will be fueled by a Waldorf salad, two Reuben sandwiches, and more potato chips than a giant mutant iguana has scales — plus my trusty jar of Maxwell House instant and its auxiliary submersible coil.

As the hotel steward wheeled the food into my room, I realized to my considerable chagrin that, having given all my folding money to Tiffany, I had no cash with which to reward his labors.

"You must be with that sci-fi convention, huh?" he asked, pointing to my Raydo. He was a freckled, klutzy kid whose large ears stuck out like radar scoops. "Did you buy that sculpture in the dealer's room?"

"Actually, I won it."

Curious now, the steward approached my desk, brushed the statuette with his greasy fingers, and pondered the inscription. "'Lifetime Achievement' — that's terrific, Mr. Thorley," he said, nervously clucking his tongue. "Not everybody manages to have an achievement in his lifetime."

"You learn your craft, you play your mummies, you collect your trophy, and then you die."

"I'm not really a sci-fi fan, but I know all about that big balloon you put on the roof. Gorgantis, King of the Lizards. Mr. Hackett isn't too happy about it. He says the darned thing should've come down this afternoon."

"I didn't put it there. Your boss should talk to the Wonderama Committee, if they haven't skipped town."

"And this is a rhedosaurus," the kid said, indicating the pewter dinosaur. "My grandfather loved that movie. He used to call me Ray the Rhedosaurus."

"This award happens to be nicknamed the Raydo. Ray Bradbury wrote the original story. Ray Harryhausen did the special effects."

"All those Rays? Really?"

"Ray Bolger did the choreography. Ray Walston played the Martian. Bob and Ray were the caterers."

"I'm Ray Wintergreen. Grampa and I watched *The Beast from 20,000 Leagues* together a month before he died."

"Fathoms, actually. Leagues is distance. Ray, my friend, I'd love to tip you, but I forfeited my last dollar to a lady of the night. Let me accompany you back downstairs, and I'll cash a check at the desk."

"That won't work. They locked the safe at eleven."

"Here's an idea. Instead of a gratuity, I'll give you my dinosaur."

"Oh, no, sir, that wouldn't be right."

"Please, Ray, I want you to have it," I said, shuffling toward my embarrassed visitor. "In honor of your grandfather."

"He was a wonderful guy, but I can't take your award."

"Of course you can." I curled my fist around the lighthouse, lifted the prize from my desk, and inserted it in Ray's grasp. "The inscription contains a typo. If I brought the damn thing home, I'd just stick it in my broom closet."

"Are you sure?"

"Absolutely."

"This is very generous of you. Mom will be darned impressed."

Fearful that his good fortune might evaporate if he lingered, Ray hugged the statuette to his chest and made a hasty exit. And so it came to pass that, like the dying dragon in Joy's story about Momoko, I surrendered my treasure to the next generation. Of course, my gestating memoir now lacked a paperweight, but the Gideon Bible in my night table drawer was easily pressed into service.

Get cracking, Syms. Drain those Bics. If you switch from amontillado to Maxwell House, you should be able to finish your memoir by 11:00 A.M., which means you'll have no trouble catching the noon shuttle to the airport or, if you prefer, the twelve o'clock window to eternity.

On Friday afternoon, twenty-four hours after the nerve-wracking *What Rough Beast* run-through, I returned to Monogram Studios with the intention of nailing Corpuscula's elaborate supercerebrum soliloquy. It was the most carefully written scene in the script — the monster's protracted and eloquent *cri de coeur* when he realizes his brain now shares cranial quarters with neuronal tissues pilfered from four different brilliant

but arguably insane scientists — so naturally Darlene showed
up to make sure Beaudine didn't fuck with her favorite lines.
For once the director decided to give the dialogue its due, and,
though he used gratuitously *noir* lighting and a meretricious
low angle, he let the great speech pour forth in one unbroken
tracking shot, the camera stalking me like a *Doppelgänger* as I
careened around Werdistratus's laboratory spouting paranoid
non sequiturs in Italian, German, French, and Spanish. I got
it on the first take, by God. When Beaudine yelled "Cut!" the
crew broke into spontaneous applause.

Thrilled with the success of the shoot and intoxicated by
the sheer visceral thrill of that greatest of all human endeav-
ors, moviemaking, Darlene and I decided a celebration was in
order. On Saturday night we splurged on front-row seats to see
Cantinflas live at the Mason Opera House, doing acrobatics
and stand-up comedy, then treated ourselves to a three-course
meal at the Brown Derby, washing down our sirloin steaks
with champagne that actually came from France. To top off a
perfect evening, we decided to enact another episode from our
erotic chapterplay about the unorthodox relationship between
Fay Wray and Gorgantis, even as we soaked the stage blood off
my monster suit in the Pacific's cleansing surf.

We parked in a secluded spot on Ocean Avenue. I climbed
into the cargo bay and slipped into my secret saurian identity,
marveling at how routine this whole business was getting to
be, my daily habit of turning myself into a dragon more fearsome than Yofuné-Nushi. After locking up the truck, I allowed
Darlene to guide me down to the beach and from there to the

sheltering pylons of the Municipal Pier. We assumed our customary postures, Gorgantis's own true love draped across his scaly arms, then headed toward the retreating tide.

The cops converged from all directions, seven frenzied shamuses, pistols drawn, flashlights blazing, fists clamped around a heavy-duty fishnet of a caliber sufficient to snare an orca. Startled, I let Darlene slip from my clutches. She scrambled to her feet and, finding the officer in charge, informed him that I was just a guy in a suit. Sergeant Loomis was unimpressed, and the next thing I knew the ponderous net was dropping over Gorgantis's massive head. So there I stood, trapped like King Kong on Broadway, terrified that my encrusted stage blood was about to be supplemented by streaming pints of the real thing.

"Freeze!" Sergeant Loomis cried, and I complied instantly. "Did the monster hurt you, ma'am?" he asked Darlene.

"He's not a monster, he's my boyfriend!"

"In my profession, you soon learn that those things aren't mutually exclusive. If he assaulted you, I want to hear about it."

Now the press arrived, an eager-beaver trench-coated reporter equipped with a spiral notebook and a pencil stub, accompanied by a photographer frantically snapping my top-secret costume with his Graflex, over and over, as fast as he could change flashbulbs — pop, pop, pop.

"Max Kettleby, *Los Angeles Examiner*," the reporter told Darlene. "I've been hot on the trail of the Santa Monica Beach Monster ever since the first sighting."

"Why won't anybody believe me?" Darlene wailed. "This is just a gag!"

"Nobody said we don't believe you, but the situation calls for a thorough investigation," Loomis replied. "When people start complaining about annoying visitations from the depths of hell, it's my job to figure out what's going on."

"This is Syms J. Thorley, the horror movie actor," Darlene said. "Did you ever see any Corpuscula pictures? He's the star, and I'm the writer."

"My operating assumption is that if it looks like a sea monster, walks like a sea monster, and bellows like a sea monster, then it's a sea monster," Loomis said.

"Syms, tell them who you are," Darlene insisted.

"I'm Isaac Margolis, recently swallowed whole by a giant mutant amphibious iguana named Gorgantis," I said.

Nobody laughed. I chuckled timorously. There are three rules of screenwriting, but only one for confronting humorless cops with drawn guns. Don't try to be funny.

"With your permission, I shall now exit this suit," I said.

"Okay, but don't make any sudden moves," Loomis said.

With excruciating caution I popped the snaps, unhitched the catches, activated the dorsal zipper, and quit my alter ego, leaving the bilious green rig standing upright in the sand. I grabbed the edge of the net and, raising my arms high, walked free.

"Hey, it really *is* Syms Thorley," Max Kettleby said.

"Who?" Loomis said.

"Syms Thorley," Kettleby said. "*Curse of Kha-Ton-Ra. Evil of Corpuscula.*"

"I'm seriously considering jamming your ass in jail, Syms Thorley," Loomis said.

"On what charge?" I asked. "Spreading panic without a license?"

"Disturbing the peace," Loomis said.

"I can explain everything," I said, praying that Darlene would now step in and explain everything.

"I'm listening," Loomis said.

"It's like this," I said. What was it like?

"Careful, Sergeant, he's a skilled actor," Kettleby said. "Don't let him bamboozle you."

"It's like this," Darlene said. "Syms and I wrote a script together."

"A sea monster script?" the reporter asked.

"*Curse of the Were-Lizard*," I said. "We got the Rubinstein sisters to make this costume for us. You know their work? *Voyage of Jonah*? *Trials of Job*?"

"Those women are geniuses," Darlene said.

"We figured that if we shopped our screenplay around in conjunction with Gorgantis himself, lots of producers would sit up and take notice," I said.

"So why have you been disturbing the peace?" Loomis asked. "Testing out the monster's scare value?"

"Before I put on my lizard for Selznick, Zanuck, Cohn, Katzman, or any other mogul — you can see the logic of this — before I do that, I need to be completely comfortable wearing the thing," I said. "How was I to know the neighbors were watching?"

"Boy, what a story!" Kettleby said, just like in the movies.

"Being a regular guy, a man of the people, and a friend of the movie business, I'm inclined to let you off with just a warning," Loomis told me. "But if folks around here want to press charges, I won't discourage them." He turned to the nearest cop and said, "Leo, take down the lizard's address, also his ladyfriend's."

Leo did as instructed. When it came to revealing her domestic coordinates, Darlene recited her sister's address in Brentwood, so we wouldn't scandalize anybody. Task accomplished, the cop looked me in the eye and said, "Hey, Mr. Thorley, would you mind if I sent you my screenplay? It's called *The Maiden and the Maniac*. You'd be great as the maniac."

"I can't wait to read it," I said evenly.

"While we're on the subject," Kettleby said, "I have a script, too, an adaptation of that amazing Franz Kafka story about the guy who turns into a cockroach. Once you take out the confusing literary stuff, it's a terrific yarn. I can see you playing Gregor Samsa."

"I'm not really a scuttler," I said. "More of a shambler."

"Believe me, you were born for the role."

"Toss it over the transom, Max. I'll be happy to take a look."

The next morning, after our usual Sunday breakfast of waffles and black coffee, I picked up the *Los Angeles Examiner* and was shocked to see my picture — and the behemoth's picture, too — luridly displayed on the front page. *Fake Sea Monster "Gorgantis" Captured in Santa Monica*, the headline screamed. *Horror Player Syms Thorley Terrorizes Neighborhood with*

"Were-Lizard" Suit, the subhead declared. Max Kettleby's article appeared on page 12, accompanied by additional photographs, including one of Darlene looking quite fetching in her bathing suit. Wonder of wonders, Kettleby got our bogus story straight. By his account, the "notorious Santa Monica Beach Monster" was merely a gimmick by which actor Syms Thorley and writer Darlene Wasserman aimed to "beguile producers into reading a horror script they co-authored." Mr. Syms and Miss Wasserman were terribly sorry for having "perpetrated an inadvertent hoax" that caused many local residents to worry that they were "about to be eaten alive in their beds," and the two B-movie celebs hoped that "all monster buffs everywhere will enjoy *Curse of the Were-Lizard* if it ever gets made."

Predictably enough, I didn't need to check in with Commander Quimby on my wrist radio, because he contacted me. He spoke entirely in tremolos. I quickly apprehended that he was furious over what he'd seen in the *Examiner*, and of course the Navy brass at China Lake were also livid. Owing to my antics, Quimby insisted, every Jap spy hiding in southern California — of which there were doubtless many, all devoted *Examiner* readers — now knew about the classified lizard rig. I countered that, thanks to my quick wits and Darlene's nimble fibs, it would never occur to a Nip agent to relay the story to his supervisors in Tokyo, since the whole foolish business was obviously just a Hollywood stunt, with no discernible connection to the American war effort.

"You've seriously compromised the security of Operation Fortune Cookie!" Quimby screamed.

"Oh?" I said. "How?"

"Admiral Strickland is beside himself! Commander Barzak, too!"

"So now there are four of them?"

"Try to get it through your head!" Quimby seethed. "You did something terribly, terribly wrong!"

"Well, the minute you figure out what it is, be sure to let me know," I said. "I've got this nifty Dick Tracy set on my wrist, and I'm always hoping somebody will call me."

"Come next Sunday, you're going to be on the road by 0700! I'll expect a radio bulletin from you at 0800 precisely and another one at 0900!"

"We Überweapons are nothing if not punctual."

Fifteen minutes later Katzman telephoned, outraged that he'd been mentioned fourth on the list of producers to whom we intended to pitch our sea monster movie, "after that schmuck Selznick, that jackass Zanuck, and that flaming anus Cohn."

"Sorry, Sam," I said. "I wasn't thinking clearly. The cops had guns. How do you like the costume?"

"It's ridiculous," Katzman said. "If Cohn wants to stick some stupid Chinese dragon in a movie and lose his shirt, that's his business."

"So you don't want to see the script?"

"What I want is for somebody to tell me why Darlene is working on this were-lizard-sea-monster-it-crawled-out-of-the-surf horseshit when she's supposed to be writing the next Corpuscula picture!"

"Occasionally an artist has to follow her heart."

"Put your girlfriend on the goddamn phone."

I shot Darlene a glance that said, *He wants to talk to you.* She reciprocated with a gaze that said, *Fix it.*

"Your favorite writer is taking a shower," I told Katzman, "but I can say for a fact that yesterday she knocked out thirty pages of *Corpuscula Meets the Vampire.*"

"Glad to hear it. As for you, looks like we can start shooting *Blood of Kha-Ton-Ra* a week from Monday."

Seeking to end the conversation on a convivial note, I told Katzman that the new Kha-Ton-Ra script was the best one yet, and if Beaudine didn't fuck it up we'd probably do some major box office. Katzman, satisfied, said "Shalom," then hung up. I consulted the kitchen calendar. The revised schedule meant that, less than twenty-four hours after sparing hundreds of thousands of U.S. soldiers the trouble of conquering Japan, I would once again be putting on my mummy bandages for the sake of the world's Kha-Ton-Ra fans. I was nothing if not versatile in those days.

Doubtless Moses was correct when, reporting on the birth of the universe, he revealed that God rested on Sunday. God, however, did not have a Hollywood career to maintain — and so it happened that I spent the entire afternoon and most of the evening typing up the final draft of "*Lycanthropus*, a screenplay by Syms J. Thorley." Throughout this interval, the telephone stubbornly refused to ring. This made no sense. How could the caliphs at Fox and Columbia not be curious about Wasserman and Thorley's *Curse of the Were-Lizard* script? Did everybody hate the Gorgantis suit as much as Katzman did?

Shortly after 9:00 P.M. I did get a call — from Dagover, of all people. He claimed he was distressed that we'd exhibited "so much pointless hostility" on the set of *Revenge of Corpuscula*, a sentiment that I assumed also applied to our six previous fractious collaborations, but he still harbored some hope that "we might become friends, or at least amicable enemies." Toward this end, he was inviting Darlene and me to "a little get-together *chez* Dagover on Saturday night."

"I have to work the next day," I said. Ending the war in the Pacific, I nearly added. "An educational film for the Army, teaching our boys how to avoid the clap. Tedious, but I need the money."

"The Army shoots movies on Sunday?"

"Their dirty little secret."

"And you're playing a gonorrhea victim?"

"So they tell me."

"*Corpuscula Meets the Whore of Babylon*, I love it," Dagover said. "Please come to my party. Darlene can make sure you don't stay up past your bedtime."

The bastard sounded so sincere I knew he was looking to screw me, but I couldn't figure out how.

"I'm expecting lots of royalty to show up," Dagover persisted. "Cohn, probably, and maybe Zanuck and Val Lewton. It might be an opportunity to sell them that sea monster movie I've been reading so much about."

No, I thought, but it sure as hell might be an opportunity to pique their interest in *Lycanthropus*. "Sounds tempting."

"The Rubinsteins built you one terrific lizard. It's got boffo written all over it."

"You think so?"

"It would be great to see you on Saturday, Syms. Eight o'clock. Bring your script. Darlene, too."

I smelled a rat, several rats, a whole Dwight Frye wet dream multitude of rats. "You're starting to win me over, Siggy."

"I'm still at Mastodon Manor, the stucco house at the corner of Curson and Lindenhurst, right by the La Brea Tar Pits. If the party gets dull, we'll dig up a woolly mammoth and have Atwill bring it back to life."

Although Darlene found Siegfried Dagover as insufferable as I did, she harbored a genuine fondness for his beleaguered wife, Esther, a corn-fed naïf from Iowa who painted innocuous watercolors and deserved better in her bed than a monomaniacal German expatriate with bad teeth. And so it happened that, when a migraine laid Darlene low early on Saturday evening, shortly after my regular six o'clock call to Quimby and two hours before Dagover's party, her distress traced as much to the canceled visit with Esther as to the affliction itself. I offered to stay home and attempt to relieve her symptoms, but Darlene insisted I attend the event, partly so I could convey her regards to Esther, but mostly because Dagover wasn't necessarily lying about Cohn, Zanuck, and Lewton being there. With hope in my heart and the *Lycanthropus* script tucked in my satchel, I climbed into the panel truck, traded grins with Gorgantis, and sped out of Santa Monica via Wilshire Boulevard, mentally rehearsing the evening's presentation to the producers and telling myself, over and over, that tomorrow's production of *What Rough Beast* mattered more to me than becoming the next big thing in werewolves.

After racing through Beverly Hills without mishap, I turned left on Ogden when I should have waited for Curson, then proceeded to learn more than I wanted to know about the cul-de-sacs south of Pan Pacific Park, but at long last I found Mastodon Manor. It would be gauche, I decided, to waltz into the party with my script in hand, so I left the satchel sitting on the passenger seat. If Zanuck or Lewton really did show up, I would turn the conversation toward Hollywood's failure to fully exploit the box-office potential of horror movies, then casually mention that we were in the vicinity of a werewolf screenplay that had me very excited.

I threw a tarp over the PRR, locked up the truck, and followed the flagstone path to the villa. A strapping blond houseboy named Rudolph, reportedly a Hitler refugee like Dagover, greeted me and took my coat. As I strolled through the burbling throng, engaging in the usual head-bobbing and smile-flashing rituals with people as indifferent to my presence as I was to theirs, I realized that to be invited to a Siggy Dagover party was to enter a select company. The guest list was a veritable Who's Almost But Not Quite Who in Hollywood. Cowboys abounded. Private eyes proliferated. Particularly conspicuous were the mad scientists. Atwill, of course, plus Lugosi and Chaney, Jr., not to mention John Carradine, whose endocrinologist in *Captive Wild Woman* was the most underrated horror performance of '43, George Zucco, who'd single-hand-edly transformed *Dead Men Walk* into a marvelously macabre oddity, and Peter Lorre, so gloriously depraved as the surgeon who grafts a murderer's hands onto Colin Clive's ragged stumps in *Mad Love*. Colin himself was probably at home, either tying one on or sleeping one off.

Noting my arrival, Dagover came sashaying across the room, weaving among the B-movie elite, his plump, unhappy spouse at his heels. Poor Esther, married to the wrong man, living in the wrong town, hosting the wrong party. This bewildered creature hadn't the foggiest idea what to say to a bunch of hard-drinking alpha males who spent their days pretending to perform blasphemous medical experiments and their nights fantasizing that they were going to give up alcohol tomorrow.

"You don't have a drink in your hand," Dagover observed. "I can remedy that."

"Hello, Esther," I said. "You may not remember me—"

"Syms Thorley," she said, brightening. "I don't see your en-chanting ladyfriend."

"In bed with a migraine."

Esther's smile collapsed like a pricked balloon, and I prom-ised myself that, before leaving Mastodon Manor, I would beg for a tour of her studio.

"I've been deputized to hug you on her behalf," I said, then threw my arms around her supple flesh like a *seringueiro* de-termining the circumference of a rubber tree.

"As I recall, you're a connoisseur of *amontillado*," Dagover said.

"Not before midnight, Montresor," I said. "I don't see Cohn anywhere. What about Zanuck?"

"They sent their regrets," Dagover said. "Lewton is planning to drop by later. Katzman, too. You brought the script, right? Your sea monster should be right up Sam's alley."

"He already passed on it. The suit doesn't work for him."

"Just between you and me, that man has execrable taste."

Obviously a case could now be made for my turning around, driving home, and nursing Darlene, but the possibility of Lewton's advent kept me rooted to the spot.

"Sam *knows* he has lousy taste," I told Dagover. "He's proud of it. The last time he went to services, he saw flaming letters blazing above the Torah. 'Thou shalt not commit art, Sam Katzman. It's bad for business.'"

As the evening wore on, I came to realize that my brush with the law had evidently been the most interesting thing to happen in Southern California that week. Gorgantis was the talk of the evening. No fewer than ten people sidled over to give me what they imagined was a good-natured ribbing. "You missed your calling, Syms. You should be sitting behind a fancy desk at Metro, cooking up publicity stunts." "I want you to know that if the cops had arrested you, I would've chipped in two bucks toward your bail, maybe even three." "Tell me the truth. You and Darlene created that sea serpent to spice up your sex life, right? All I want to know is, does it work?" Eventually my ribs couldn't take it anymore, and I sought out Esther, imploring her to lead me upstairs to her studio, a wish she was only too happy to grant.

During the seven years since I'd last seen Esther's paintings, her drafting skills had improved, her brushwork had become masterful, and her sensibility had turned morbid. Where once her walls had glowed with soothing still-lifes of flowers and sea shells, I now confronted a cavalcade of grimy, wasted men who looked prepared to commit any act short of bathing, interspersed with landscapes whose unifying subject was the failed disposition of the dead. To my immediate left, the earth of a Haitian cemetery fractured beneath a crop of rising zombies. On a nearby easel, a dozen gossamer ghosts streamed forth from a crumbling mausoleum, headed for a come-as-you-aren't party somewhere east of oblivion. At the back of the studio, a moldering mob of former churchyard tenants marched into a nearby abbey bringing bad theological news.

Watercolors remained the artist's medium of choice, and I could not help admiring the skill with which she'd pressed those intrinsically cheery hues into the service of irremediable gloom. This was not the Esther Dagover *oeuvre* I knew, but I liked it.

"Oh, *there* you are!" her husband called from the doorway. "Isn't Esther's work simply *stunning* these days?"

"She deserves her own gallery," I said.

"You think so?" Esther said.

"Giant bipedal mutant amphibian iguanas never lie," I said.

"Huh?"

"If you can tear yourself away from these wonderful things, we're about to screen a classic," Dagover said.

"Which one?" I asked.

"Val Lewton asked me that same question twenty minutes ago."

"He's here?"

Dagover answered with a burst of anxious chatter. What was eating my rival? He seemed to be stuck in some sort of Gentile seder, convinced that this night was different from all other nights. "Lewton's not here, no. He called. We talked. *The Cabinet of Dr. Caligari*. Val's never seen it. Smart money says he'll show up. Did you know my cousin's in the cast? Lil Dagover. She plays the ingénue. *Ingénue* is an anagram for *Genuine*, the title of Wiene's subsequent picture."

"Just as Szilard is an anagram for lizards," I noted.

"What?"

By normal Hollywood standards, Mastodon Manor was an unimpressive estate, no swimming pool, no tennis court, no Roman baths, not even a wet bar, but it did have a basement movie theater complete with upholstered seats and — to avoid any hiatus during reel changes — dual 35mm projectors housed in a soundproof booth. Before a Dagover party ran its course, the guests were normally treated to one of the contraband films that had accompanied him on his flight from the Nazis. His collection included a print of almost every picture made by UFA during the twenties. Whatever his shortcomings, Dagover had apparently smuggled the whole of Weimar cinema out of Berlin just in time to prevent Hitler from putting it to the torch.

Did I want to see *The Cabinet of Dr. Caligari* again? Not really. Under most circumstances, I would've gladly forgone

Wiene's aggressively eccentric movie for more time with Esther and her disaffected cadavers. Was Dagover lying through his teeth when he hinted that Lewton might be on the way? Probably — and yet there now came to my ears the steady rush of that Shakespearean tide which, taken at the flood, leads on to fortune.

"Be honest, Syms," Esther said. "My visions are too bleak these days. They belong on the cover of *Weird Tales*."

"Even as we speak, brilliant men contemplate the immolation of countless innocent victims through fire-breathing, city-stomping behemoths," I told her. "Compared with the desolation in the skulls of our admirals, your visions belong on the cover of the *Saturday Evening Post*."

Exuding an uncharacteristic unctuousness, Dagover escorted me down three flights of stairs to his subterranean Rialto, its walls decorated with posters for *Metropolis*, *Die Nibelungen*, and other UFA epics, then guided me to the best seat in the house, a lounge chair covered in maroon velvet. The place was practically empty. Evidently *Caligari* held little appeal for the guests at this particular party — or perhaps they'd demurred on patriotic principle, the filmmakers being, after all, Krauts. Chester "Boston Blackie" Morris and his wife had shown up, plus Sidney "Charlie Chan" Toler, Tom "The Falcon" Conway, and Warner "Crime Doctor" Baxter. Lewton was nowhere to be seen.

Barely concealing his disappointment over the low turn-out, Dagover introduced the film with forced zeal, urging us to take seriously the claim of the writers, Carl Mayer and Hans Janowitz, that their work should be read allegorically, with the mountebank Caligari symbolizing the politicians who'd maneuvered Germany into the Great War and the somnambulist Cesare representing the young men who'd been hypnotized into imagining the conflict would be steeped in glory. The film, in short, was an artistic brief for pacifism, a kind of *All Quiet on the Expressionist Front*, with Walter Röhrig's crooked sets instead of Erich Maria Remarque's bloody trenches.

As *Caligari* unspooled, Dagover insisted on serving me a glass of my beloved amontillado, and a second glass after that, and the consequent inebriation did much to rehabilitate the movie in my eyes. Where once I'd dismissed *Caligari* as a shotgun marriage of cinema and painting, I now beheld a near masterpiece, each jagged image drawing the audience ever deeper into the mind of the schizophrenic protagonist. This was precisely the direction in which the film medium had not gone, the evocation of aberrant psychological states through unabashedly artificial décor, and I found myself wishing that dozens of similarly audacious pictures had followed.

With my third glass of sherry, my critical faculties evaporated altogether, and I realized I was drifting in and out of consciousness. I stayed awake long enough to see the angry mob kill Cesare, and then I became dead to the world.

Slowly, languorously, my left eyelid lifted into my skull, followed by the right, a process as protracted as the somnambulist's great black orbs flickering open at Caligari's command.

My carotid arteries spasmed. My throat throbbed. A mad scientist had amputated my tongue and grafted a slug in its place. Gradually I became aware of four astonishing facts. I was still in Dagover's private theater, my body lay sprawled across a divan in the corner, somebody had stolen my wrist radio, and it was nine o'clock in the morning, or so my pocket watch claimed, unless, of course, it was nine at night — a dubious theory, since that would mean I'd been unconscious nearly twenty-four hours.

"Good morning, Syms," Dagover said, thereby clearing up some of my confusion. He was straddling a chair beside the projection booth, his arms folded on the headrest, contemplating me with his most remorseless Werdistratus gaze. Rudolph hovered in the background, waiting to do Dagover's bidding like Noble Johnson anticipating Lugosi's next directive in *Murders in the Rue Morgue*.

Nine A.M. There was still enough time for me to make the four-hour drive to China Lake and star in the momentous matinee performance of *What Rough Beast*. "I'm not supposed to be here. I'm supposed to be" — for all his flaws, Dagover was surely not an enemy spy, but I decided to maintain my cover story anyway — "on my way to Burbank, so I can do that VD film for the Army."

"I remember," Dagover said. He wore a green satin smoking jacket. Balanced on his lower lip, his unlit cigarette moved up and down like a semaphore as he talked. "And Monday you start shooting *Blood of Kha-Ton-Ra*. Don't worry — I already spoke to Darlene. She knows you spent the night here."

"Give me my wrist radio back. I need to call the gonorrhea people and tell them I'll be late for the shoot."

"You mean that thing's real? I thought you got it out of a Cracker Jack box."

"Give it back."

"'All in good time,' as I told you in the final reel of *Flesh of Iron*."

I made a rigid arc with my thumb and middle finger, using these fleshly calipers to massage my aching temples. "I feel like Corpuscula. My brains have burst out of my skull."

"Had a little too much amontillado, did we?"

"It sure packs quite a wallop."

"One might almost imagine I drugged you," Dagover said.

Stretching my arms, extending my legs, I took an inventory of myself. Muscles, tendons, ligaments, eyes, ears, jaw: all my thespian assets were in working order. I was ready to act my heart out in Hangar A. Had Dagover said *drugged?* Huh? What?

"You drugged me?"

"I wouldn't put it that way," Dagover said, lighting his cigarette.

"You just did."

"I needed to make sure you remained behind after the other guests left. The door to my movie theater is locked, and the key resides in a secret location. It would not be an exaggeration to say you are my prisoner."

"Have you gone mad?" I said, another line from *Flesh of Iron*.

"A plausible theory," Dagover said. "The evidence is persuasive. Not only did I put a sedative in your sherry, I'm about to train a gun on your heart." From the pocket of his smoking jacket he produced a derringer, which he pointed in my direction. "It's loaded."

"Fuck," I said.

"My terms are simple. This were-lizard of yours is precisely what my career needs right now. The suit is marvelous, and the premise sounds even better. Our protagonist starts out a Karloffian goody-goody — right? — looking to cure cancer with lizard glands — am I getting warm? — but he feels obligated to experiment on himself, and the injections turn him into a reptilian horror — I'm hot now, yes? — living in sewers and crashing into the heroine's boudoir. Obviously the script demands a virtuoso performance, and I'm the man to deliver it."

"There is no script," I said.

"Shut up," Dagover said. "I haven't finished. The instant I snap my fingers, Rudolph will fetch my typewriter. I'm going to dictate a cover letter to him, which you will sign forthwith." He took an elegant Continental drag on his cigarette. "'To whom it may concern. Darlene Wasserman and I wrote the attached screenplay, *Curse of the Were-Lizard*, with Siegfried Dagover in mind. So profound is our commitment to seeing Mr. Dagover in the lead, we have given him our Gorgantis costume to do with as he pleases. While I might accept a small part in the film, I shall not consider playing the monster under any conditions. Yours truly, Syms J. Thorley.' Well, my friend, do we have a deal?"

"There is no Gorgantis script."

"Let's make sure you understand the stakes," Dagover said, stroking his derringer. "If you don't give me this plum, I'm going to keep you here through Tuesday night, which means you'll miss the first two shooting days on *Blood of Kha-Ton-Ra*, which means Sam will fire you, which means he'll hire *me* to play the mummy, and we can't have *that*, can we?"

"Siggy, you've got to let me go right now! You don't understand! *There is no Gorgantis script!* There's only this thing called *What Rough Beast*, which Brenda wrote under a Navy contract after some scientists at a secret Mojave lab started feeling guilty about breeding psychopathic incendiary lizards as biological weapons!"

"*My* insane actor impersonation is good, Syms, but *yours* is better."

"I'm not kidding! Operation Fortune Cookie!"

"My ass."

Dear reader, dear God, what other choice did I have? Surely we can agree that I was obligated to tell Dagover the whole story: the horrendous behemoths, Ivan Groelish's petition to President Truman, the failure of the Midget Lizard Initiative, Obie's model city, the recent arrival of a Japanese delegation on American soil. And so I did. I unbagged every confidential cat and spilled each classified bean. Naturally Dagover greeted my tale with disbelief, but his doubts began to dissipate after I showed him my ID badge and explained that the New Amsterdam Project was a code name for the Knickerbocker Project. His skepticism vanished altogether after Rudolph went off to reconnoiter the manor grounds and returned with the news that the fleet in the driveway indeed included a U.S. Navy panel truck whose cargo bay contained the lizard suit.

"Now that I've heard the whole story, I must admit it makes more sense than what I read in the *Examiner*," Dagover said. "I kept asking myself, 'Where did Thorley get the money to commission such a classy monster rig?'" He firmed his grip on the derringer. "I guess the Navy would be pretty unhappy to hear you've been blabbing about their iguanas. Don't worry, Syms, I'll keep everything under my hat."

"I appreciate that," I said. "So do the thousands of American boys waiting to invade the Japanese mainland."

"Sounds like the Knickerbocker people are counting on you for a performance to beat the band," Dagover said.

"You got that right," I said. "So if you'll please put down your gun, return my Dick Tracy set, and unlock the door, I'll be on my way."

"Not so fast, Syms. Something just occurred to me. Whoever wrecks that Shirazuka model this afternoon is going to end up a kind of war hero — right? — with lots of honors and Hollywood contracts to follow. I'm thinking the savior in question might as well be me."

"No, Siggy. Bad idea."

"I'll put on the costume and get Rudolph to drive me out to Inyokern. 'Poor old Syms Thorley,' I'll tell your Admiral Yordan. 'He's sick as a dog. But you needn't worry, sir. Siegfried K. Dagover is here to save the day.' It's all so delicious, don't you think? A Kraut with his own print of *Triumph of the Will* ending World War Two. There's some real poetry in that, if you ask me."

"What you're saying is crazy, and you know it. You haven't rehearsed. You haven't studied Brenda's script. The suit has all sorts of quirks."

"Script? What script? Gorgantis wades ashore, finds a god-damn Willis O'Brien city full of slant-eyed fanatics, burns it down, fade-out."

"Siggy, please, I've put a hundred hours into preparing for this part. You could never bring it off. If the demonstration shot fails, there won't be any accolades for you. You'll spend the next forty years hanging your head in shame."

"I'm already hanging my head in shame. You think I'm going to get a fucking Oscar for *Revenge of Corpuscula*?"

"Besides, I've got a much better scheme." Did I? Indeed — not a plan I liked, but it was the lesser of two evils. "Send Rudolph back to the truck. He'll find a script on the passenger seat."

"You said there wasn't one."

"A completely different project, the best werewolf script ever, authored by yours truly. Except I *didn't* write it, Siggy. *You* did. Just retype the title page. '*Lycanthropus*, a Screenplay by Siegfried K. Dagover.' Tell Cohn and Zanuck and Lewton you always knew you had a script in you, and here it is."

"You're trying to trick me."

"I'm on the level, you Jew-hating goyische Nazi schmuck! This is your fucking destiny, Siggy! This is opportunity knocking on your wooden head!"

"If I were you, I wouldn't talk that way to somebody who was pointing a gun at me."

"Cross my heart, Baron Ordlust will write your ticket to the fucking Horror Hall of Fame! Long after everybody's forgotten about Karloff and Lugosi and — what's-his-name? — Thorley, they'll remember Siegfried Dagover!"

My nemesis furrowed his brow, pocketed his derringer, and dispatched Rudolph to fetch the masterly scenario in question. He returned within five minutes, bearing my *Lycanthropus* satchel.

"This better be good," Dagover informed me.

"Promise me one thing," I said. "Read it quickly. Even as we speak, the Jap delegation is having breakfast at China Lake."

"I'll read it at whatever velocity suits my mood."

"Jesus Christ, Siggy."

"Big man in my church."

"Do you have even the *remotest* idea of the geopolitical implications of keeping me locked up here?"

Instead of answering, Dagover announced that he was going to his first-floor study, the place where he did all his best work.

"Oh, and one more thing," he said, climbing the stairs. "If I decide to let you go" — he inserted the key in the lock — "you have to give me your solemn word."

"About what?"

"About joining the Siegfried Dagover Fan Club."

"My pleasure," I said between gritted teeth. "While I'm at it, I'll recruit Darlene. I didn't know there was a Siegfried Dagover Fan Club."

"There isn't," Dagover said, twisting the key with the emphatic theatricality of Werdistratus switching on a dynamo. "You're going to start one. Naturally I'll expect you to be the first president, and the vice-president, too. Maybe we can get the Rubinstein girls to design the membership cards."

V

FOUR O'CLOCK in the morning. The hour when, it is said, more people die in their sleep, dream of illicit love, and write bad lines of movie dialogue than at any other time of day. Like Sam Katzman supervising one of his Monogram epics, I have managed to keep this memoir on schedule, largely because the last chapter flowed from my pen without any interruptions, no misdirected call girls, no room service deliveries, no visitors from Porlock, no ravens bearing intimations of mortality. Instant coffee courses though my veins, flushing old memories into consciousness from the deepest reaches of my brain.

Only once did the torrent of ink stop. The fault was mine. Shortly after composing the scene in which the Santa Monica police capture Gorgantis on the beach, I took a bathroom break and, instead of heading directly back to my desk, absently flicked on the television. I spun through the cable channels and — presto — there it was, *Atom-Age Lycanthropus*, 1957, the eighth and final entry in the successful series that had started eleven years earlier when B-movie actor Siegfried Dagover peddled a clever little werewolf script to Harry Cohn at Columbia. Until the day the project went before the cameras, I'm sure Dagover feared I would step forward and claim credit for the screenplay or, worse, the delicious concept at its core:

Baron Basil Ordlust, the aristocratic thrill-seeker who travels the world in quest of the man-beast whose bite will transport him to hidden realms of decadent ecstasy. But a bargain is a bargain, even in Hollywood. When I handed Siggy his break-through role, I meant that he should keep it.

Crisply lensed by Karl Freund and smartly directed by Edgar G. Ulmer, the present scene was infinitely depressing — and not just because that should have been *me* up there on the screen, and instead it was Dagover, suavely solidifying his mystique as the Ronald Coleman of horror movies. What really both-ered me was the undeniable skill with which the bastard had milked the moment. The scene found Ordlust in the Mexican jungles, hiding out in the temple of the local jaguar-goddess and trying to convince her fleshly avatar, lasciviously played by Ruth Roman, to favor him with her fangs. An entirely standard situation for the series, but Dagover and Roman brought so much erotic energy to the encounter you could practically see the pheromones fluttering around them like moths. Gesture by gesture, intonation by intonation, Dagover was doing ev-erything right.

To this day, film scholars wonder why Columbia's Lycan-thropus was the only monster from the classic Hollywood pantheon to last into the fifties, when audience tastes in genre horror shifted radically from the gothic to the cosmic. I suspect this success can be traced to two facts: Baron Ordlust never shared the screen with Abbott and Costello, who belonged ex-clusively to Universal, and Harry Cohn insisted that his writers work radioactivity or an alien visitation into every Lycanthropus installment, preferably both. On first principles, were-wolves and flying saucers have little in common, but Cohn's loyal pencil-pushers rose to the occasion.

Consider *Lycanthropus in Space*, in which the Baron convinces a team of rocket scientists to send him to Venus, planet of shape-shifting carrot-women. Or *Galactic Lycanthropus*, in which an extraterrestrial scientist lands on Earth and attempts to extract the life essence from Baron Ordlust, whose *joie de vivre* is exactly what's needed back on Procyon-5. When that particular entry was being cast, in February of 1955, my career had bottomed out, so Cohn and Dagover threw me a bone, the role of the phlegmatic alien. I acquitted myself well, but I was better in *What Rough Beast*.

It would be an understatement to say that Commander Quimby wanted my head on a platter, my ass in a sling, and my guts on a loom after, having recovered my wrist radio from Dagover, I called him and confessed that a rival had drugged me the previous night at a Hollywood party, with the result that the demonstration shot might have to be delayed by as much as an hour. Back then there were no intercontinental rockets bearing thermonuclear warheads, but Quimby still went ballistic, asserting that Yordan would probably be forced to improvise delaying tactics, "such as challenging the Jap delegation to a sake-drinking contest," a potentially disastrous development that could easily make them "too sloshed to take the annihilation of Shirazuka seriously." Before shutting off his radio, Quimby calmed down and started thinking strategi-

cally. He told me he would order the California Highway Patrol
to permit all Navy panel trucks zooming north on Route 14 to
break the speed limit and any other statutes that might prevent me from reaching China Lake on time.

No sooner had the behemoth and I motored away from
Mastodon Manor than a fresh disaster struck. Glancing at the
gas gauge, I saw that it was within a hair's-breadth of E — E for
egregious oversight, execrable planning, extraordinary stupid-
ity. Today was Sunday. All the service stations would be closed.
Gasoline, gasoline everywhere, and not a drop to fuel the end of
World War Two. Even my friend Gorgantis betrayed me. Three
days earlier I'd drained all the petroleum from his tail during
target practice in an Inglewood automobile graveyard, inciner-
ating rocks and cacti, the derelict cars themselves having been
carted off long ago as scrap metal for the military.

I hadn't a prayer of reaching Inyokern, but I figured I could
limp back to Mastodon Manor. My calculation proved correct. Just as I was pulling into Dagover's driveway, the engine
gasped, groaned, and conked out entirely. When I explained
the situation, Dagover proved uncharacteristically sympathetic — he was still giddy over his theft of the *Lycanthropus*
script — and he cheerfully lent me his Duesenberg, which happened to have a full tank.

Mindful that we could probably use the backup lizard in
the Quonset hut at the Château Mojave, I considered ditch-
ing the PRR. Being unfamiliar with the duplicate's quirks and
kinks, however, I soon thought better of the idea, so I strapped
Gorgantis to the roof of Dagover's car like a canoe. Shortly

after zooming past the L.A. city limits, I started wondering if I should get on my Dick Tracy set and instruct Quimby to tell the state police to ignore all Duesenbergs bearing dinosaurs. But I really didn't want to deal with the commander again. If a trooper pulled me over, I would simply explain that I was delivering the monster to a diner in Bakersfield, so they could use it to advertise their newest specialty, the Behemoth Burger. Should the officer still insist on giving me a ticket, I would flash my ID badge and tell him to stop fucking with the course of American history.

After three hours of running stoplights, exceeding the speed limit, and otherwise indulging in deplorable citizenship, I pulled up before the Château Mojave, parking between Whale's Rolls Royce and Joy's convertible. Admiral Yordan's chauffeur was pacing around the staff car, treading a circular furrow in the sand. Four other sailors stood at attention beside the canopied troop transport, ready to deliver Gorgantis to Hangar A. I scrambled out of the Duesenberg, accorded my PRR a quick glance — evidently it had survived the trip without mishap — and dashed into the *atelier*.

Eyes greeted me, a baker's dozen, Yordan being a cyclops, presumably lodged in their owners' skulls but nevertheless exuding a disembodied quality. Thirteen detached, discrete, extremely angry eyes.

"I should have you keelhauled!" Yordan screamed.

"Bad enough you got the lizard's picture in the paper — but *this* is outrageous!" Dr. Groelish cried.

"Do you realize you're on in thirty-five minutes?" Joy asked.

"You let us down," Gladys said.

"We're very disappointed," Mabel said.

"Most unprofessional of you," Obie said.

"You'll never work in this desert again," Whale said.

"Boil me in oil!" I shouted. "Tear out my teeth! But right now we've got a war to win!"

Yordan scowled, perhaps annoyed that he hadn't thought of that line himself, then ordered the transport detail to retrieve the PRR. As the sailors carried Gorgantis into the *atelier*, the admiral explained that he was about to rejoin the Jap delegation, presently finishing their luncheon in the officer's mess. Before taking off in his staff car, he made a tactical decision to clasp my shoulder, offer me an affirming smile, and wish me luck.

While Mabel replenished my oxygen cylinder and fueled the flamethrower, Gladys suited me up with her usual cool professionalism, refusing to let her spleen find its way to her fingers. Halfway through the process, Whale reached out with both hands and squeezed my left claw, while Joy accorded my torso a similarly reassuring hug. Perhaps their affection was entirely pragmatic, intended only to shore up this unreliable actor in whom so many of their personal ambitions were invested, but I preferred to believe they'd forgiven me.

Dr. Groelish revealed that the unveiling of the sedated giant lizards had been a great success, with Marquis Kido, Deputy Minister Kase, Chief Secretary Sakomizu, Information Director Shimomura, and their translator struggling unsuccessfully to banish the infinite awe from their normally impassive faces.

The exhibition of the tranquilized dwarfs had also gone well, with the emissaries apparently getting no inkling that when fully awake these creatures were pussycats. Thus far the day's only unexpected development was the delegation's request for permission to document their mission on motion picture film. Anticipating the Navy's assent, the emissaries had brought along two professional cinematographers and a pair of silent 35mm Kinarris acquired years ago from their German allies.

"Did Strickland say yes?" Whale asked.

"Reluctantly," Dr. Groelish replied. "He forbade them to use artificial lighting on the giants, lest they become aroused."

"Their footage of Blondie, Dagwood, and Mr. Dithers will be underexposed," Whale said, "but the attack on Shirazuka should turn out fine, Obie's lighting being brilliant in both senses of the word."

"Thank you," Obie said.

"So the behemoths really unnerved them?" I asked.

"Marquis Kido wanted to know how many such weapons we had in our arsenal," Dr. Groelish said. "I could hear the anxiety in his voice. Naturally Strickland didn't tell him."

"Secretary Sakomizu insisted that only barbarians would inflict such monsters on cities," Joy said. "Barzak shut him up with the Rape of Nanking."

"Minister Kase predicted that, whatever the outcome of the war, the prevailing powers will engage in a lizard race," Dr. Groelish said. "Strickland responded that the outcome of the war was not in doubt, and Mr. Kase should stop pretending otherwise."

"Mr. Shimomura asserted that a carefully choreographed air strike, artillery barrage, or armored attack would easily lay the behemoths low," Joy said. "It was all bluster, of course."

"Done!" Mabel said, shaking a final drop of gasoline into my tail.

"*Voilà!*" Gladys said, activating the last zipper.

"Four minutes ahead of schedule!" Dr. Groelish said.

"All hail the Monogram Shambler!" Joy said.

"Sink their fleet," Whale instructed me. "Smash their planes. Crush their artillery. Melt their tanks. Break a leg."

Entombed in the bathyscaphe, my neoprene habitat resounding with my rubbery breaths, my stomach undergoing colonization by a hundred epileptic butterflies, I inevitably thought of the agonies suffered by the nameless narrator of Poe's "The Premature Burial." Although the tale ends happily, with the protagonist getting cured of his catalepsy, most of the story concerns his morbid anticipation of untimely interment. I knew the key passage by heart, having made it the centerpiece of my unsuccessful audition for a role that ultimately went to Lugosi, the diabolical Legendre in *White Zombie*, and now snippets returned to me like bits of flotsam washing up on a beach.

"The unendurable oppression of the lungs — the stifling fumes of the damp earth — the rigid embrace of the narrow house — the blackness of the absolute night — the unseen but palpable presence of the conqueror worm."

Admiral Yordan recited his opening monologue, insisting

that for even the bravest warrior there could be no honor, only meaningless obliteration, in taking the field against a raging behemoth. This time around, the speech made me squirm. Our job was not to tell the Japanese what to think about the lizards, but to show them that when such weapons were unleashed, what followed was unthinkable.

The music began. Today Waxman's dissonant and distressing overture sounded didactic, a sermon spun from notes instead of words. Next came more of Yordan's folderol, his pretentious conjuration of Gorgantis from the depths of the sea.

"The doors of hell open! The beast rises! Doom comes to Shirazuka!"

As the grand "Gorgantis Theme" resonated through the bathyscaphe, I flooded the chamber, squeezed through the hatch, and assumed my crouch. Should I open the oxygen cylinder? No, I decided. Better to hold that invaluable commodity in reserve, using it to keep from blacking out at the height of the conflagration.

Abruptly I stood erect, crashing through the surface of the bay. The water came up to my waist. I was not a happy monster. We had insulted the emissaries. My isinglass peepholes disclosed the moonlit harbor with its seven anchored warships, riding the tide. Our scale-model Japanese fleet now seemed like yet another affront, gratuitously reminding the delegation that their nation no longer had a navy. What was the intended subtext of Brenda's script? Was she saying to our visitors, "Look, foolish warriors, even if the gods gave you a new armada, it would avail you nothing"?

JAMES MORROW

I began with the carriers, scooping the *Akagi* out of the water — in reality, the Japs had lost that one at Midway — while simultaneously seizing the *Shinano*, which had actually been torpedoed and sent to the bottom on its shakedown cruise. Fighters and dive bombers spilled into the bay like pawns tumbling from an upended chess board. As in the rehearsal, I smacked the two flight decks together. Waxman's percussionist provided the cymbal crash. I hurled the fractured carriers aside with the insouciance of a chimpanzee tossing away a banana peel. The twisted hulks hit the water and vanished.

Smoke gushing from their stacks, searchlights blazing from their bridges, the remainder of the fleet steamed out to meet the threat, two destroyers, two heavy cruisers, and the late, great dreadnought *Yamato*, mysteriously resurrected following her heroic suicide run of the previous April. The five warships encircled Gorgantis, ravenous sharks moving in for the kill. A thunderous volley shook the bay. As the musicians played the cue called "Floating Fortresses," barrages of shells pelted my leathery skin like horizontal sleet. Mindful of Whale's insistence that we should give the enemy false hopes, I pretended to reel under the fusillade — which wasn't difficult, for Obie had loaded the warships' guns with far more cordite than necessary, so that half the BB's ripped through the PRR and then my street clothes, nicking the bare skin beneath. Thanks to Obie's red-dye blisters, streams of blood were soon coursing down the monster's chest, glistening in the moonlight like trails left by iridescent slugs. I squeezed my roar-bulb. Gorgantis bellowed and swished his tail, stirring up a tsunami in

Toyama Bay that nearly caused the remainder of the fleet to founder.

Balling my claws, raising them high, I launched my counterattack. Relentlessly I hammered the destroyers, staving in their hulls and sending them instantly to the bottom. Next I vented my wrath on the heavy cruisers, pounding both warships until the roiling deep swallowed them forever. When it came to dispatching the *Yamato*, I decided to improvise. Clasping the vessel in both claws, I extended my arms and relaxed my grip. The dreadnought plummeted. My rising foot broke its fall, instep crashing into keel, and the *Yamato* became instantly airborne, flying across Shirazuka, glancing off Mount Onibaba, and hurtling into the blackness beyond.

Having won the Battle of Toyama Bay, I now began my trek toward shore, when suddenly a burst of unscripted violence intruded upon the demonstration. To this day I'm not sure how I received my wound. Probably I stepped on the fractured deck of a sunken warship, the jagged edge tearing through the behemoth's right heel, penetrating my tennis shoe, and burrowing into the flesh beyond. I squeezed my roar-bulb, so that Gorgantis's mighty cry drowned out my screams of pain.

Clumsily I heaved myself onto dry land, my warm blood pooling inside the breached cavity of the lizard's leg. I hoped Whale was correct when he said a vulnerable monster would best serve our purpose, because for the rest of the show the emissaries would get just that, Gorgantis the humbled, the crippled, struggling to stay upright. Keep going, Syms. You can do this. Move your goddamn flat feet, first the good one

— yes, yes — next the right — oh, shit — next the left — yes — the right — shit — the left, the right, left, right. You are the undying dragon, the immortal maggot, the unconquerable worm.

Even in my tormented condition I could appreciate the luminous beauty of a nocturnal passenger train, flashing through the Far Eastern darkness to Waxman's scherzo, its blazing lamps illuminating the conversations, card games, and reading matter of a thousand weary travelers. But the universe of Überweapons is bereft of aesthetics. For an enraged lizard, the many-windowed creature riding the trestle was merely a rival reptile. It must be torn from its tracks and devoured.

I squeezed my roar-bulb. As Gorgantis bellowed and swished his tail, crushing warehouses, ship berths, gantries, and other waterfront installations, his serrated teeth parted, and I crammed the great luminous serpent into the gaping maw. The monster chewed, mashing a dozen coaches and their helpless riders, while the rest of the train — locomotive, tender, unswallowed cars — dribbled from both sides of his mouth like a string of sausages.

Directly ahead stretched one of Obie's most exquisite creations, a row of high-tension power lines marking the border between the harbor and the city proper. Gorgantis charged into the mesh, his feet uprooting the towers like so many croquet hoops, his claws slashing through the cables like an actor batting away cobwebs on a Monogram sound stage. Showers of sparks arced across the moonlit sky. Per Whale's direction, I pretended to suffer a near electrocution — not a difficult deception, for, as with the Japanese naval guns, Obie had overdone it, supplying the cables with far more juice than he'd used in the rehearsal.

It had been a night to remember, but now the moon set, the sun rose, and the birds awoke, as if roused by Waxman's ominous "Dawn" cue. The bleeding beast gathered his strength. His wounded heel throbbed. Again he roared. And the evening and the morning were the first act.

Perhaps the pain in my foot prevented me from thinking clearly, but an unfathomable compassion now seized my reptilian soul. How many brave Japanese sailors had I drowned by the light of the moon? How many night watchmen had I killed? How many insomniac strollers, graveyard-shift stevedores, and travelers on the Imperial Railway?

No, Syms. You've got it backwards. Heed Jimmy Whale's wisdom. Go down to the muck. Become the worst of all possible Calibans, for only then will the Knickerbocker behemoths stay where they belong, torpid on the floor of China Lake. Become a true son of Sycorax, bile pouring from your heart, curses spewing from your lips. "'As wicked dew as e'er my mother brushed with raven's feather from unwholesome fen,'" I growled under my breath, "'drop on you both!'"

Cruelty renewed, depravity regained, I shuffled through the ruins of the harbor, my hurt foot leaving a bright red ribbon on the terrain. The wound still smarted, but I sensed that the clotting process had begun. Peering through my peepholes, I surveyed the remaining targets: the immediate city, its slumbering suburbs, and finally, north of the Kosugi River, the mountains where dwelled holy Hirohito, descendant of the sun goddess Amaterasu. Beyond the peaks, I dimly apprehended another realm, the world of Operation Fortune Cookie, including the two Japanese cinematographers, cranking away with their silent Kinarris, plus the four emissaries — my captive audience — sitting high above in their sealed balcony, and farther still, in the darkest corner of Hangar A, the orchestra, working to unnerve the delegation with Waxman's discordant "Inferno Theme."

Stay in character, Syms. You are the id-thing, the hag-spawned horror, hurling invectives at your despicable master. "'All the infections that the sun sucks up from bogs, fens, flats on Prosper fall,'" I hissed to myself, "'and make him by inch-meal a disease!'"

Done. I'd touched bottom. Here in the belly of the behemoth I'd met my primal Caliban. The urge to burn — to burn, decimate, slaughter, and slay — rushed through me like the strongest sexual desire a vertebrate might ever know. But first I must switch on my oxygen. I set my palm against the lizard's navel, creating a friction fit between my skin and the valve. Deftly, subtly, I rotated the handle, then leaned back on my haunches and waited for the lizard's interior climate to change.

Nothing. No whisper of escaping gas. No cool rush of air. Was the mechanism broken? Had Gladys and Mabel accidentally installed an empty cylinder? Don't panic, Syms. Be a serene killing machine, a mellow abomination, a plague as pacific as a corpse.

I had no choice but to proceed with the dismantling of Shirazuka — and so I did, aligning Gorgantis's snout with the heart of the city and squeezing the burn-bulb. A great gush of fire jetted from the dragon's mouth, and soon a dozen office buildings, apartment complexes, and department stores were in flames. I squeezed the roar-bulb. Releasing a demon scream, Gorgantis whipped his tail and swept a jumbled mass of cars, buses, trolleys, and flaming rubble into an uptown neighborhood. For the next ten minutes the behemoth pursued this remorseless strategy, alternately crisping the city with his fiery lungs and battering it with his juggernaut tail. I did not neglect the personal touch. Reaching down, I grabbed a bunch of helpless citizens and, as in the rehearsal, popped them into my jaws. The Lilliputians lodged in the back of Gorgantis's throat like a cluster of mutant tonsils.

Just as I feared, the holocaust soon created an intolerable atmosphere inside my PRR. Saltwater erupted from my scalp and rushed into my eyes. Smoke leaked through the BB holes in my hide. My every breath was a great wheezing gust. I coughed convulsively. When the Imperial Air Force appeared, they met an enemy much weaker than the Syms Thorley of the run-through. Today they faced a sweat-blind and half-suffocated mortal, reeling from anemia.

The dive bombers came at me from every point of the compass, raining exploding firecrackers on my head, shoulders, chest, and thighs, even as the fighter planes shot blood blisters into my neck and groin. Obie had not stinted on the red dye, and Gorgantis was soon bleeding from a hundred fresh wounds. Given my dazed and anguished state, it was the fairest fight so far, doubtless recalling for the delegation the epiphanies of Pearl Harbor and the Indian Ocean. But the day, I vowed, would belong to the lizard. A blind behemoth was still a behemoth, a preternatural force before whom every rock, tree, river, hill, and valley in creation trembled. Transcending my distress, I lashed out in full fury, arms flailing, claws thrashing, and so it was that, bomber by bomber, fighter by fighter, I swatted the Imperial Air Force out of the skies, sending each stricken, smoking, shrieking plane on its final flight, a vertical journey to oblivion.

Methodically I removed my right hand from Gorgantis's claw, then pulled the hem of my undershirt free of my trousers and pressed the cotton fabric to my eyes, sopping up the sweat. I scanned the rubble that once was Shirazuka. Before my remorseless gaze, a dozen fires smoldered. Phantom lamentations reached my ears, the screams of the maimed, the threnodies of the bereaved, the wailing of widows and orphans. And the grieving and the mourning were the second act.

Had it occurred on the great island of Honshu and not in a U.S. Navy airplane hangar, the defense of the Imperial Palace would have earned its rightful place among the most brilliant deployments in military history. No conventional force could have taken Mount Onibaba without causalities running into the hundreds of thousands, so astutely had General Anami arrayed his Chi-Ro tanks and field artillery along every pass, cliff, and switchback between the foothills and the lofty fortress.

But a Knickerbocker behemoth was not a conventional force. Dr. Groelish's Überweapon precluded heroic stands and noble sacrifices. Such affectations had no place in the universe of pornographic ordnance.

Like some vast, swirling, terrestrial maelstrom, Gorgantis came storming through the Chiaki Mountains. The Japanese threw everything they had at the invader. As the ferocious engagement continued, the lizard sustained myriad wounds, so that his scaly exterior showed more blood than skin. And still he kept coming, shambling over the sharp peaks, carrying the war to His Majesty, charging to the frenzied beat of Waxman's cue titled "Death of an Emperor."

Inside the PRR, nothing was going right. Torrents of sweat gushed from my brow, stinging my eyes like vindictive hornets. As with the Toyama Bay engagement, over half of the Japanese BB's had penetrated my hide — evidently Obie had doubled the amount of cordite he'd used for in Hangar B — peppering my flesh with tiny cuts and admitting still more smoke. A coughing fit wracked my frame. The wound in my foot had opened up again. I could hear the rubbery slosh of blood against the lizard's sole. Expressionist shadows flickered through my skull. A squidish ink suffused my mind.

At last I could see the palace, shining in the sun, guarded by fearsome armored divisions and bristling gun batteries. Repeating a bit of business Whale had introduced during the run-through, I heated the Chi-Ro tanks until they became pliable and, snatching them up two at a time, knotted their gun barrels together — a grotesquely cartoonish gesture, the Axis

Meets Bugs Bunny. My assault on the field artillery was equally decisive, though lacking the wit with which I'd dispatched the tanks. I merely used the full fury of my dragon breath, turning the cannons into shimmering metallic blobs that dotted the mountains like patches of snow.

Now came the moment of truth, the hour of reckoning, the battle of the gods. On the Japanese side: the divine, benign, beatific, saintly, murderous, bloodthirsty Hirohito. On the American side: a different sort of deity, an eschatological reptile with few if any illusions about himself. Unless some equally powerful dragon came to Hirohito's aid, the ghost of Yofuné-Nushi perhaps, rising from Toyama Bay, the god-emperor's fate was sealed.

The most violent passage in Waxman's score reverberated through Hangar A, the one titled, with a nod to the late FDR, "Righteous Might," and as the cue built to its climax, I brought both my fists down hard on the palace. The fortress withstood the blow. Again I pounded. Fissures appeared, snaking across the plaster of Paris walls. A third blow. The fortress crumbled. Obie's stage-blood packet exploded. Crimson cataracts rushed down the slopes like lava from a volcano.

For the beast's triumphant exit, Waxman reprised the majestic "Gorgantis Theme," and thanks to its stirring strains I found the strength to quit the scene without losing consciousness. As I lumbered toward the Japanese cinematographers, bloody but unbowed, they nervously overcranked their cameras — which meant that, developed and projected, the footage would appear in slow-motion. I kept on going, stumbling over cables, staggering past the orchestra. Suddenly the rear door swung open, admitting a dazzling shaft of desert light. I passed through the blessed portal to the glistening sands beyond, where Whale, Obie, and the twins stood waiting to hoist me into the troop transport. Once I was safely ensconced beneath the canvas canopy, Dr. Groelish and his academically ravishing daughter emerged from the shadows.

"You were stupendous," Joy said, flourishing a $5,000 check, the remainder of my salary.

"I believed every minute of it," Obie said, scrambling aboard along with Whale and the Rubinstein sisters.

"Your greatest performance ever," Dr. Groelish said as we sped away from Hangar A.

"You found your Caliban," Whale said.

"You balled the jack," Gladys said.

"You shot the moon," Mabel said.

"I cut my foot," I said. "I've lost a lot of blood. Take me to the infirmary."

VI

A DOUR AND DRIZZLY Monday has come to Baltimore. Raindrops skitter down my windows like translucent beetles in some unspeakably poetic science fiction movie by Andrei Tarkovsky. The management of this Holiday Inn has reacted to October's chill by cranking up the heat, and so far all my attempts to counter their zeal by fiddling with the thermostat have failed. So here I sit in my stuffy little room, determined to complete this memoir before my sins get the better of me and I undertake my rendezvous with gravity.

Breakfast arrived a few minutes ago, at 7:45 A.M. to be precise, just as I'd finished fleeing the scene of my crimes against Shirazuka. My dealings with room service have been promiscuous of late. Pancakes, a cheese omelet, hash browns, English muffins, butter, marmalade, orange juice, coffee. The condemned man's last meal is a feast.

Strangely enough, the breakfast steward was the same Ray Wintergreen who brought last night's dinner. When I asked why he was working such grueling hours, he explained that, shortly after leaving my room, his newly acquired pewter rhedosaurus in hand, he'd learned that a fellow employee had called in sick. Ray had immediately agreed to work overtime, happy in the knowledge that the extra pay would increase the fund he'd earmarked for replacing his mother's ten-speed bicycle. Before a dump truck ran over her beloved Schwinn, the sprightly woman had enjoyed pedaling on country roads all the way to the Mason-Dixon line and back.

"The world would be a better place if more people did that," I said.

"Rode bicycles?" Ray said.

"Bought them for their mothers."

"Mom's an early riser," Ray noted, carefully transferring the breakfast tray from his cart to my desk. "I called her an hour ago. She said to thank you for the rhedosaurus. She'd forgotten what a kick Grampa got out of that movie."

"Once again I find myself in the awkward situation of having no gratuity to give you."

"Don't worry about it," the exhausted steward said, opening his mouth to maximum diameter and drawing in a breath. "A Raydo is worth a thousand tips."

I yawned reciprocally. "By an odd coincidence, we've both been up all night."

"My shift ends at noon, and then the Wonderama people are paying me twenty bucks to help them get their Gorgantis balloon off the roof. Next week they're renting it to an Apple Butter Festival in Pennsylvania, and then it goes to New York City for the Thanksgiving Day Parade. Shall I pour you some coffee?"

I grunted in the affirmative. "If I were in charge of this hotel, I'd buy the balloon from the convention the instant Macy's is finished with it. Such a magnificent Gorgantis will attract swarms of customers."

"You're absolutely right," Ray said, filling my Holiday Inn mug. "All weekend people have been stopping by and asking about our dinosaur. They like the idea of us becoming more family-oriented."

"And what could be more family-oriented than a fire-breathing demon who roasts people alive?"

"But Mr. Hackett, he hates the thing," Ray said, sidling toward the door. "If you want my opinion, he doesn't have a good head for business. He told the convention he wants that darned balloon out of here by noon, not one minute later, or he's going up on the roof with an ice pick." He opened the door and stepped into the hall. "It's been great getting to know you, sir. Enjoy your breakfast."

Enjoy my breakfast. That is precisely my intention. We who are about to die know how to live.

When I finally got to inspect the foot injury I'd acquired while wading through Shirazuka harbor, my first and only war wound, it looked every bit as dreadful as I'd feared. The resourceful Rubinstein sisters soon managed to improvise a bandage from Whale's ascot, a stopgap measure that I'm convinced kept me from bleeding to death. By the time we reached the China Lake infirmary, the cut had started clotting again, so that all the Navy surgeons had to do was give me a Novocain injection, clean out the gash, close it with sutures, and shoot me full of penicillin.

Stalwart professional that I am, I defied the doctors' wishes and had Joy drive me to Hollywood the next morning. At noon I reported for duty on the set of *Blood of Kha-Ton-Ra*. If you ever see the picture, an experience I don't recommend, note how the mummy's limp is more severe than in his previous outing, *Curse of Kha-Ton-Ra*. A similar hobble characterizes my appearance in the last two alchemical creature movies, *Corpuscula Meets the Vampire* and *Son of Corpuscula*.

And so it began, the great waiting. Minute by minute, hour by hour, day by day, the scattered company of *What Rough Beast* was convulsed by anticipation. I scrupulously scanned every issue of the *Los Angeles Examiner*, listened devoutly to H. V. Kaltenborn's broadcasts, and routinely called Commander Quimby on my Dick Tracy set. Nothing, nada, zero, zip — not one news bulletin suggesting that our demonstration shot had sent Marquis Kido, Chief Secretary Sakomizu, Deputy Minister Kase, and Information Director Shimomura running to Emperor Hirohito with tears in their eyes, insisting that he spare his nation a behemoth attack.

Meanwhile the Pacific War ground on. Throughout the horrific month of June, kamikaze pilots continued their suicidal missions against the advancing American fleet, the Army Air Force relentlessly firebombed Tokyo, and the sands of Okinawa soaked up the blood of 72,000 American corpses, 131,303 Japanese dead, and 150,000 civilian victims. During that same dreadful interval, the Manhattan Project got back on track when Oppenheimer's team concocted an implosion-triggered device fueled by plutonium, a design they successfully tested on July 16 in the desert near Alamogordo, New Mexico. They named this primal atomic explosion Trinity. In the name of the Father, and of the second sun, and of the profane ghosts of a thousand immolated kangaroo rats, horned lizards, Gila monsters, and kit foxes. Amen.

From the instant we heard about Hiroshima and Nagasaki, a question began haunting the *What Rough Beast* troupe. Did Harry Truman reason that, because the stomping of Shirazuka had not translated into a Japanese surrender, an exhibition of the Manhattan Project's equally dramatic fruits would prove futile as well? For what it's worth, history vindicates us on that score. All existing records suggest that, despite their favorable response to the China Lake Petition, Truman and his advisors were — with one exception — never sympathetic to the idea of an A-bomb demonstration, neither before nor after it became clear that Operation Fortune Cookie had not met expectations. The dissenter was Assistant Secretary of War John J. McCloy, who favored full disclosure of the new weapon. Every other member of the Interim Committee of the Manhattan Project feared that if the A-bomb proved a dud, the Japanese would merely be emboldened to dig in and wait for the Allies to get sick of the war. And even if the sneak preview came off without a hitch, the Interim Committee reasoned, the witnesses would probably fail to grasp the true military import of what they were seeing. Finally, in the Committee's view the element of surprise was vital: only a bolt from the blue, with consequent massive casualties and unimaginable suffering, would shock the Imperial Government into accepting the draconian sur-render terms of the Potsdam Proclamation.

A second question soon took root in our company's collective imagination. How would we have felt if Truman had rebuffed General Groves's appeal for two successive A-bomb attacks and instead honored Admiral Strickland's request that the behemoths be transported to Honshu's coastal waters without delay? My guess is that our guilt would have been even greater, if such a thing is possible. True, the Gorgantis suit had always elicited a certain affection among the China Lake troupers, but the monsters themselves were manifestly among the most horrendous weapons ever to appear on Earth. Whatever quantity of anguish Leslie Groves's raids caused the people of Hiroshima and Nagasaki, it was surely no greater than the devastation that Blondie, Dagwood, Mr. Dithers, and their cousins would have inflicted on those same cities, or any other targets that caught Strickland's fancy.

Six months into the American Occupation of Japan, I visited Commander Quimby in his subterranean office, and he told me everything he'd learned about the activities of Kido, Sakomizu, Kase, and Shimomura following their visit to China Lake. From the handful of captured documents that General MacArthur's staff had declassified thus far, Quimby concluded that our demonstration shot had shaken the four witnesses to the core, but soon afterwards they'd begun convincing each other that giant fire-breathing mutant iguanas weren't so terrible after all. By the time they made their report to Emperor Hirohito and Prime Minister Suzuki — an oral account supplemented by their silent 35mm footage of the lake-dwelling adult behemoths and the dwarf's attack on the miniature

Shirazuka — the emissaries had decided that their nation could defeat the monsters. And so, when Hirohito and Suzuki in turn informed General Anami and his staff about the strategic reptiles, their presentation lacked urgency, and the militarists had no trouble dismissing these biological anomalies as a species of conventional ordnance, easily countered through artillery and civil defense.

I was grateful for one, and only one, of Quimby's findings. According to the first round of declassified documents from Tokyo, it never occurred to Kido, Sakomizu, Kase, or Shimomura that the dwarf who'd savaged the model metropolis was a man in a suit. While the newspaper photographs of the Santa Monica Beach Monster may have given the Japanese espionage community momentary pause, one can safely infer that Max Kettleby's *Los Angeles Examiner* story had never come to the four emissaries' attention.

When I returned to China Lake to join Joy in burying the second generation of dwarves — despite their severe progeria, Huey, Dewey, and Louie had lived for almost a year after V-J Day — she did her best to cheer me up, but I was inconsolable. Mired in some irreducible amalgam of self-pity and bitterness, I'd become convinced that failure of Operation Fortune Cookie traced to aesthetic defects in our production of *What Rough Beast*.

"Don't be ridiculous," Joy said, adorning Huey's grave with a Santa Rita prickly pear cactus.

"Brenda's script had certain virtues," I said, "but it was ultimately banal."

"The problem wasn't Brenda's script. The problem was the insanity of the Japanese high command."

"Obie's model city should've been more intricate."

"Nonsense," Joy said, honoring Dewey with a beavertail prickly pear cactus.

"Whale's direction was flat. Waxman's score was schmaltzy. The lizard suit wasn't demonic enough."

Joy decorated Louie's final resting place with a California barrel cactus. "If it had been any more demonic, Satan would've sued the Rubenstein twins for appropriating his persona."

"My acting lacked conviction. Stanislavski would not have been impressed."

"Rubbish, Syms. You gave the performance of a lifetime. I was there."

"No doubt about it, Joy. We dropped the ball."

For what it's worth, Operation Fortune Cookie actually did reduce casualties in World War Two. The last time I saw Quimby, sometime in 1952, he informed me that throughout July of 1945 and the first week in August, the Imperial Ministry of Homeland Security had tripled the watch along the shores of Honshu. The Japanese leaders knew that, having squandered what was left of their navy in the *Ten-ichi-go* sortie, they could not destroy any American subs that might appear towing sedated behemoths, but they could at least try to evacuate the targeted city before the monsters were awakened and unchained. Thanks to our demonstration shot, as many as two hundred civil defense workers who might otherwise have been in the heart of Hiroshima on the morning of Monday, August

6, 1945, were prowling nearby coves, binoculars in hand, looking for periscopes poking above the waves, and so they were
spared when a uranium-fueled hell burst over the city. Three
days later, another one hundred and seventy-five civil defense
personnel found themselves at a safe distance when a plutonium bomb leveled Nagasaki. So you might say that *What
Rough Beast* saved almost four hundred lives — even as it failed
to deliver 177,000 Japanese from death by blast, incineration,
and acute radiation sickness, and another 300,000 from turning into *hibakusha*, "explosion-affected persons," the walking
wounded with their lacerations, burns, mental disorders, and
incipient cancers.

To this day, I'm not sure why the Navy's Bureau of Teratoid Operations was shut down immediately after the Pacific
War ended. I know only that the ink was barely dry on General Umezu's signature when the Pentagon ordered Admiral
Strickland's group to exterminate the three adult behemoths
by deoxygenating China Lake, then destroy the twenty em-
bryos through whatever means might prove most efficient.
Upon receiving word that Blondie, Dagwood, and Mr. Dithers
had drowned, the War Department arranged for the Knickerbocker Project to remain classified well into the next century.
Because Strickland's budget had always been piggy-backed
onto the Manhattan Project, it wasn't difficult for the Truman
White House and subsequent administrations, Republican
and Democratic, to act as if the giant reptiles had never ex-
isted. For the sake of the historical record, though, I must note
that the Los Alamos bombs actually cost the taxpayers a mere

one and a half billion dollars. The remaining five hundred million went into iguanas of mass destruction.

Did our military leaders come to view the behemoths as a technology so awful, so disgusting, so counter to every value that civilized nations hold dear, that even the most hawkish could not abide their continued cultivation? I doubt it. Conversely, did the *What Rough Beast* fiasco convince the Pentagon that the monsters weren't quite awful *enough*, and it would be better to specialize in the indubitable horror of nuclear weapons? A reasonable argument, but it's more likely that the Joint Chiefs simply didn't want to deal with the debilitating interservice rivalry that would surely follow if the Army and the Navy each had its own distinctive way of ending the world.

Or perhaps the Pentagon's considerations were primarily tactical. A behemoth is a capricious thing, after all, its behavior unpredictable compared with the purely technical problem of building an atomic bomb and delivering it to a target. For whatever reasons, the Lizard Age, I am happy to report, ended almost as soon as it began.

Unable to face another swatch of fabric or vat of foam rubber without thinking of Gorgantis, the Rubinstein sisters left Los Angeles early in 1946. They moved to Wyoming, opened a kennel, and set about breeding Labrador retrievers as seeing-eye dogs. The last I heard from Gladys, sometime in the late sixties, Mabel was dying of heart disease, the kennel had been sold, and they were living on Social Security in Bakersfield.

Brenda Weisberg remained in the movie industry for another six years, but she never wrote anything as memorable as *The Mad Ghoul* or *The Mummy's Ghost* or, for that matter, *What Rough Beast*. According to her biographer, the perspicacious Jeri Smith-Ready, Brenda seemed "curiously depressed and distracted" during the final phase of her Hollywood career, which saw her contributing DOA scripts to such humdrum pictures as *King of the Wild Horses*, *Ding Dong Williams*, *When a Girl's Beautiful*, and *My Dog Rusty*. Did Brenda ultimately find peace? Such was the impression I got from a postcard I received in 1962. By her laconic account she was back in the Arizona of her childhood, happily married and "keeping my demons at bay by writing and directing for the Phoenix Little Theater."

James Whale, too, found peace, though of a more static and controversial variety. In 1957, at the age of sixty-seven, the director of *Frankenstein*, *Bride of Frankenstein*, and *What Rough Beast* drowned himself in his swimming pool. His decision may be plausibly attributed to several factors, among them loneliness, poor health, and the frustration of a truncated career, his last feature being *They Dare Not Love* of 1941. I'm convinced that Whale's homosexuality had nothing to do with his suicide, and equally persuaded that, if our behemoth demonstration had worked, he would have held on much longer — painting, sketching, planting his garden, tending to his memories.

For many years Willis O'Brien managed to remain active in the industry. Throughout 1947 he supervised his protégé

Ray Harryhausen on the intricate stop-motion animation that makes *Mighty Joe Young* such a watchable romp. I cannot help regarding the climax of that picture, in which the huge gorilla helps rescue the young residents of a burning orphanage, as Obie's attempt to give Operation Fortune Cookie the denouement it deserved. He couldn't save the children of Hiroshima and Nagasaki, but at least he could deliver dozens of fictional foundlings from a similarly fiery death. Alas, after rising to the occasion of *Mighty Joe Young*, Obie was stricken with a bad case of post-Gorgantis stress syndrome. He lost his ability to sell himself, and no more prestigious assignments came his way. His work on *The Black Scorpion* and *The Giant Behemoth* was impressive as always, but the films themselves lacked magic, causing little stir upon their release. In 1960, two years before his death, Obie endured the final humiliation, when Irwin Allen recruited him as an "effects technician" on a wretched reincarnation of the picture that had made his career, *The Lost World* of 1925. Allen's inexcusable movie did not contain even one second of stop-motion, merely live lizards decked out in horns and spikes, pathetically impersonating dinosaurs. The last instance of Obie's handiwork to reach the big screen graces that mirthless exercise in celluloid elephantiasis, Stanley Kramer's *It's a Mad, Mad, Mad, Mad World*. Obie contributed to the violent climax, animating eleven articulated puppets representing members of the all-star cast, dutifully hurtling them, as the script required, to near-certain death from a wildly oscillating fire-engine ladder. Such is the span of this gifted man's career, a sorrowful sweep from a beguiling *Lost World* to a meaningless *Mad World*. It's a sad, sad, sad, sad arc.

As for the post-war Syms Thorley, he started off the new decade as a monster in trouble, drinking too much, sleeping too little, despairing too frequently, tumescing too seldom — the worst possible man for Darlene to have in her life. I was dismissed by three talent agents in as many months. On those rare occasions when I got to sleep, my subconscious insisted on tormenting me with mushroom clouds and irradiated children. I lost weight, friends, money, hope.

Walking out on me was Darlene's second wisest choice of 1952, the first being her decision to relocate to Manhattan and join the television revolution, a move that soon led to her successful anthology series *Shock Street*, hosted by a drug-addled Bela Lugosi. Back in those days, you may recall, almost everything that appeared on your personal cathode-ray tube was either a film-chain broadcast from Hollywood or a real-time presentation from New York. Among the morbid fascinations of those crude but endearing *Shock Street* programs was watching poor Lugosi dying before your eyes on live television.

For the next three years I was a Jewish Blanche Dubois, dependent on the kindness of strangers, not to mention the charity of acquaintances, the gullibility of relatives, and occasionally even the benevolence of enemies, as when Dagover gave me a role in *Galactic Lycanthropus*. But then something extraordinary occurred. Late in 1955 I received a letter from Saburo Miyauchi, head of production at the nascent Kokusai Pictures in Tokyo. Mr. Miyauchi informed me that his company was about to enter the American market with a dubbed version of *Yofuné-Nushi, Creature of Wrath*, a sci-fi spectacle featuring a radioactive prehistoric lizard. Every shot of the titular monster, Mr. Miyauchi confessed, had been salvaged from the black-and-white 35mm silent footage that "the China Lake emissaries brought back to Japan two months before the war ended." He had two reasons for writing. First, he wanted to offer me ¥50,000 — about five hundred dollars — as compensation for my appropriated performance. Second, because *Yofuné-Nushi, Creature of Wrath* had been so popular in Japan, "even among the explosion-affected persons," he hoped I would accept ¥200,000 to appear in the sequel, *Yofuné-Nushi Strikes Again*, which would feature "the backup version of the lizard suit that figured in our first monster film, the original costume being unusable owing to the rips and burns it acquired during your U.S. Navy's presentation to the Imperial Delegation in June of 1945."

I have yet to learn exactly how the Kokusai executives deduced that the dwarf behemoth who effaced the miniature Shirazuka was actually an actor in a suit. Perhaps after the war somebody sent Mr. Miyauchi the *Los Angeles Examiner* photos of the Santa Monica Beach Monster, and he put two and two together. One thing is clear. Kokusai didn't pay the Defense Department a single yen for the duplicate PRR. The costume had been a bribe, pure and simple, given to the Japanese moguls on condition that they keep mum about the Knickerbocker Project.

In my reply to Mr. Miyauchi, I informed him that, before

signing a contract, I would have to speak with my agent — by which I meant that, thanks to this deal, I could now probably convince some predatory ten-percenter to represent me — but I told him I believed this was the start of a productive partnership. In the final paragraph, I offered my opinion that American audiences would never warm up to a picture called *Yofuné-Nushi, Creature of Wrath*. If I were a Japanese movie magnate, I would call the English-language release of my sci-fi epic *Gorgantis, King of the Lizards*.

Three weeks later I flew to Tokyo, where I joined the ranks of *gaijin*, foreigners, laboring in the grotty but honorable fields of *kaiju eiga*, monster movies. Although no reputable L.A. agent was interested in my new career, I soon acquired the local services of Yozo "Johnny" Mosura, a combination talent scout and Tokyo League baseball bookie. Despite the omnipresent saki and beer I managed to stay relatively sober, limping my way through nine Gorgantis epics, three of which I wrote myself.

After two decades, Kokusai's *kaiju eiga* empire ceased to be profitable, but by then I was sufficiently solvent to repatriate myself. I bought a house in Malibu and became a bourgeois beach bum, bedeviled by drink, haunted by the ghosts of China Lake, but still finding reasons to get up in the morning. In time I discovered a new vocation, putting my talent for melodramatic plotting to lucrative use. Encouraged by my New York literary agent, Rachel Bishop, I churned out a half-dozen paperback horror novels for Aardvark Books, all ostensibly written by somebody named Sean Prince, my pseudonym's pseudonym.

About ten years ago, both of my pasts — Monogram Pictures living legend and *kaiju eiga* superstar — caught up with me, and I became a darling of the monster-movie convention circuit. Every month would bring a new celebration: Monster Bash, Cinemacabre, Charnel Carnival, Shadowflix, Wonderama. I held forth on panels, did public interviews, made guest-of-honor speeches, and presented my 35mm slide-show on the art of suit acting. At some point during any given appearance I would start ranting about the *hibakusha*. The fans learned to put up with it. What choice did they have? When Corpuscula, Kha-Ton-Ra, or Gorgantis talks, the true believer listens. As the years went on and the conventions began blurring into each other, I found myself making indiscreet allusions to the Knickerbocker lizards, but mostly I stuck to the atomic bombing of Japan.

"The instant that doctors in the Hiroshima and Nagasaki hospitals began reporting thousands of fatalities from a mysterious plague, General Groves undertook to persuade the American public that the A-bomb attacks had involved no appreciable radioactive fallout. A famous photograph showed the general's personal driver, a young soldier named Patrick Stout, standing in the Hiroshima bomb crater, smiling up at the camera. Twenty-four years later, at the age of fifty-three, Stout died of leukemia."

Every time I told that story, the convention attendees greeted me with glassy-eyed stares. They'd come to hear about Corpuscula, not blood cancer.

"Most historians agree that Hirohito's 'sacred decision' to

demand total capitulation of his generals was undergirded by two extraordinary events: the Soviet Union's entry into the Pacific War, and the atomic bombing of Hiroshima. Does this mean that the attack on Nagasaki was unnecessary? It's difficult to say, but two facts are incontrovertible. First, General Groves obsessively arranged for the Nagasaki bombing to occur as quickly as possible after the Hiroshima raid, on the dubious theory that nothing short of a one-two punch would get the enemy's attention. Second, on the morning of August 8, two days following Hiroshima and twenty-four hours before the destruction of Nagasaki, Foreign Minister Shigenori Togo sat down to confer with Hirohito, only to learn that, because of the devastating new weapon, the Emperor had decided to terminate the war posthaste, thus sparing his people further suffering."

These remarks also elicited blank expressions from the *kaiju eiga* faithful. The fans perked up only when I mentioned in passing that Togo's son-in-law had helped to found Kokusai Pictures.

"It's worth remembering that, beyond using atomic bombs to force a Japanese surrender, Truman and his Secretary of State, James Byrnes, also hoped the new weapon would help the United States constrain Soviet ambitions after the war. 'It seems to be the most terrible thing ever discovered,' the President wrote in his diary, 'but it can be made the most useful.' Thus did Truman and Byrnes become charter members of the Machiavellian club that today includes the architects of President Reagan's nuclear arms buildup: unlettered and parochial men promoting incendiary devices whose true nature they do not understand — the quintessential peasants with the ultimate torches."

A few Gorgantis aficionados seemed interested in this point, knowing as they did that certain prominent strategists in the Reagan Administration harbored illusions of moving beyond the Cold War into a glorious and only mildly radioactive era of nuclear victory over the Soviets. But most fans simply looked at their watches.

"As Susan Sontag argues in her brilliant essay, 'The Imagination of Disaster,' science fiction films enable us to participate in the fantasy of living not only through our own deaths, but also the death of cities and the destruction of humanity itself. In Sontag's memorable phrase, such movies are 'in complicity with the abhorrent.'"

Of all the points I liked to make at the conventions, that one went over the least well with the fans.

I must admit that my acceptance speech following the Wonderama Awards dinner was the most pompous and didactic yet. Beyond my usual screed about the *hibakusha*, my topic was Harry Truman's convoluted post-war statements concerning Hiroshima. Even I was embarrassed by the irrelevance of my remarks — an inarticulate attack on inarticulateness — and I left the banquet hall before finding out who'd won the raffle for the Gorgantis suit replica.

"I made the only decision I ever knew how to make," Truman famously asserted in one of his carefully scripted reminiscences. What does that mean, exactly? Did Truman see himself as a professional decision-maker with a narrow specialty, the choice between destroying and not destroying Japanese cities? What is the distinction, exactly, between being *unable* to make any other decision and *never having been able* to make any other decision? Have Überweapons made coherence obsolete? As we become ever more complicitous in the abhorrent, will eloquence, lucidity, and reason itself—

Wait. Damn. Someone's at the door. Crap.

I'm not sure who I was expecting to find on the threshold of Room 2014. Ray the rhedosaurus fan? Tiffany the hooker? Darlene Wasserman, wanting to give the relationship another chance?

I certainly wasn't anticipating Gorgantis, but there he stood, my reptilian *alter ego,* throwing his head back in a mighty roar while sweeping the hall carpet with his tail. The human inside the suit introduced himself as Eric Yamashita, the convention attendee who'd won the raffle on Saturday night. His reasons for darkening my door were twofold. First, he wanted to tell me how much he enjoyed my acceptance speech at the banquet, especially my expression of sympathy for the *hibakusha.* Second, he'd inadvertently imprisoned himself in the costume, and he was hoping that I recalled enough about its complicated zipper system to liberate him.

I invited my young fan into the room.

"I cannot tell you how fortunate I feel that this suit has come into my possession," Gorgantis said.

"Would you like me to autograph it?" I asked.

"Extrication will be sufficient. But not immediately. At the moment I am happy to be inside. I feel blessed by the lizard's enveloping presence."

"So did I, once upon a time."

"Two years ago I joined the Germantown Society of Friends," Gorgantis said. "I now run their most active committee, the Greater Philadelphia Coalition to Halt the Arms Race."

"A Japanese Quaker?" I said.

"Rather the way you're a Jewish Buddhist," Gorgantis said.

"I'm not a Buddhist."

"Ah, but you are, Mr. Thorley, even if you don't know it. Your philosophical remarks on Saturday night gave you away."

I told Eric there was some lukewarm coffee left over from breakfast. Would he care for a cup? He replied that, oddly enough, he was a devotee of lukewarm coffee, and he would be happy to accept my offer once free of the costume.

"I don't think of sci-fi fans as political activists," I said.

"When somebody tells you he loves monster movies, you're learning very little about him. I hope to make this magnificent lizard as famous a symbol for the abolition of nuclear weapons as Smokey the Bear has become for the prevention of forest fires. The Reagan Administration has thus far managed to ignore apartheid, poverty, pollution, and the AIDS epidemic, but I won't allow them to deny the behemoth."

"I assume there's no flamethrower in there."

"Probably not, but in case it's got one, I should still be allowed to keep the costume," Gorgantis noted with maximum reptilian acerbity. "Isn't that why we have the Second Amendment?" He bellowed and swished his tail. "The time has come for me to hatch."

I ran my hands all over the rubbery fabric, as if frisking the lizard for a concealed weapon. This particular Gorgantis incarnation did not perfectly replicate the prototype, but I still located all the relevant catches, snaps, and zippers. Five minutes later, a sweating and smiling young man stepped out, wearing blue jeans and a Phillies baseball jersey. He was remarkably handsome, reminiscent of Kojiro Hongo from *Daikaiju Ketto Gamera tai Barugon*, which graced American screens in 1966 as *War of the Monsters*. If Jimmy Whale were here, he would've fallen instantly in love.

"Before I go, I must tell you why nuclear abolition means so much to me," Eric said. "My favorite aunt was a *hibakusha*."

"I'm sorry."

"Until two years ago, Megumi Yamashita lived with us, or, to be more accurate, passed her living death with us. We lost her to thyroid cancer. She never talked about Hiroshima, but one day I found a long letter she'd written to her brother in Kyoto. It went on for forty pages."

"Maybe you should publish it," I said, pouring lukewarm coffee into a hotel mug. "I have a good agent these days."

"She told of the blinding flash and the black rain. She described the burned survivors staggering toward the river. Their eyes had melted in their skulls. My aunt wrote that a cyclone made of screams tore through the city that day. The people were crying for their mothers, their children, their gods, their deaths. Most especially they cried for water."

"The radiation." I passed Eric his mug of tepid brew. "It causes intolerable thirst."

"Their skin was coming off in sheets, like wax dripping from a candle."

"I've seen the pictures." Kha-Ton-Ra's flesh was likewise a tenuous organ, but he had all those bandages to hold it in place.

Eric sipped coffee. "Somehow my aunt made it to the hospital. She'd been trained as a nurse, so she wanted to volunteer. She wasn't prepared for what she found. How could she be? A little girl with no arms. A little boy whose head had become a charred blister. Another boy whose lips and cheeks had vanished, so you could see his broiled gums and all his teeth. Wasn't the Hiroshima bomb called Little Boy?"

"And Nagasaki was Fat Man."

My visitor was weeping now. "Another little girl, no more than five. Her name was Yukiko. All the skin on her back had fallen away. She kept crying 'Mommy! Water! Mommy! Water!' My aunt tried to give her some water, but Yukiko was thrashing too much from the pain. She died without seeing her mother."

From the pocket of his jeans Eric produced a neatly folded white handkerchief. He daubed the tears from his eyes and swabbed the mucus from his nose. A silent minute elapsed. I ate the last English muffin. My visitor finished his coffee.

"On the way up here I met the steward to whom you gave your Raydo," Eric said at last. "Am I to infer a dark meaning from that gesture?"

"Bull's-eye. You smoked me out."

My visitor dragged his Gorgantis suit back toward the entrance to my steamy room. "In your speech at the banquet, I heard a terrible despair."

"Call it my tribute to Yukiko."

"Yukiko would not be honored."

"My inspiration is Claude Eatherly," I said. "The pilot who flew the weather plane that found the skies over Hiroshima sufficiently clear on the morning of August 6, 1945. His personality was never the most stable, but Little Boy broke him completely — psychiatric disorders, criminal behavior, suicidal impulses."

"But he never killed himself."

"He was a braver man than I."

Eric wrapped his fingers around the door handle. "Mr. Thorley, I beg you." He withdrew his hand, jammed it in his pocket. "This can't be right."

"You're talking to a *hibakusha.*"

"I think not."

"Oh, yes, my friend. A *hibakusha.* Have no doubt."

It took me a half-hour to convince Eric Yamashita that nothing he could say or do would deflect me from my path. At last the young abolitionist took up his lizard rig and left. Once again I am alone.

I know what this moment expects of me. Its demands could not be clearer. I am to find redemption in Eric's brief visit. Because I moved him so deeply, I should now resolve to keep on attending sci-fi movie conventions, haranguing the fans about Hiroshima and Nagasaki, thereby enlightening a small but significant minority.

But I can no longer live in the moment. I can only live in the past, an intolerable location, and the future, which I shall find habitable only to the degree that I am not there.

My bags are not yet packed. The noon shuttle will leave without me. Like Mr. Poe, I am weak and weary. I must sleep. I am weary of god-emperors and their obscene obliviousness to the blood in which their divinity is soaked. I am weary of the God of Leslie Groves and Harry Truman, that atom-splitting deity who one day presented the general and his President with a gift from on high, or so they believed. I am weary of the God of my Fathers and his meager regard for mothers, including the one who gave birth to Yukiko. I am weary of the incarnate God who makes such a moving cameo appearance at the end of Obie's *The Last Days of Pompeii* but who sat paring his nails while Vesuvius vaporized twenty thousand people. I am weary of the fission bomb, the fusion bomb, and — coming soon to an arsenal near you — Ronald Reagan's neutron bomb. Our world suffers from a surfeit of the sacred, and I shall not be sorry to leave it.

The next time you have a chance to watch the original *Corpuscula*, stay with it till the end of act two, which finds me slipping furtively into the front parlor of Castle Werdistratus. It's Darlene's best piece of writing ever, and probably my best job of acting, and for once Beaudine knew where to put the camera.

The room is empty but for the scientist's young son, Anton, who sprawls on the carpet playing with his toy freight train, its spring-driven steam locomotive coupled to a box car, a tank car, a gondola, and a caboose. A half-dozen wooden horses occupy the gondola. When Corpuscula sits down beside the train, Anton is startled but not frightened. The boy winds up his locomotive and releases it. Corpuscula deliberately places his leg across the track. The train derails. Horses fly in all directions. Corpuscula laughs.

After scolding the monster, Anton restores the train to the track, winds up the locomotive, and sends the horses on their way. Once again Corpuscula causes a wreck — but this time it's the *monster* who carefully, oh, so carefully, places each bruised and battered horse back in the gondola.

The boy allows Corpuscula to wind up the locomotive. The train begins its circular journey. Suddenly Werdistratus appears, shotgun in hand, and chases his creature into the night.

And that is how I wish to be remembered, friends. I am Corpuscula, savior of horses. *Sayonara.*

While there would be a certain poetry in giving Syms Thorley the last word, especially since that word was Sayonara, *the editors wish to add a coda. We are pleased to have presented the fullest narrative yet published concerning the Knickerbocker Project. Though some people may call our actions unpatriotic, even treasonous, we felt duty-bound to shed light not only on an arcane chapter in American history but also on the motives* behind Thorley's jump from the twentieth floor of a Baltimore Holiday Inn.

His suicide attempt was famously unsuccessful. By an astonishing turn of fate, the flatbed truck bearing the partially deflated Gorgantis balloon passed beneath the window just as the hapless actor plummeted toward the parking lot. The behemoth was supine, so Thorley must have glimpsed the grinning jaws right before he hit the stomach. He bounced. Slamming into the hotel wall, he cracked his skull, with resultant cerebral trauma. To the day he died — from old age as much as anything — on March 18, 1993, in a second-rate Santa Monica nursing home, he never uttered a single word, nor did he lose his fixed, seraphic smile, so unlike the monster's yet perhaps inspired by it.

Despite his catatonia Thorley enjoyed a steady stream of visitors, among them Joy Groelish, Darlene Wasserman, Eric Yamashita, and Esther Dagover, who'd divorced Siegfried in 1962 and subsequently married a Beverly Hills art dealer. No doubt Sam Katzman and Brenda Weisberg would have also paid their respects, but the former had passed away in 1973, and the latter was too ill to travel. At one point Tiffany Nolan flew in from Baltimore. Crouching over his wheelchair, she told Thorley how, as she was leaving the Holiday Inn with her autographed video of Gorgantis vs. Miasmica, she was approached by Wilbur McKee, a twenty-six-year-old Wonderama attendee. Emboldened by their mutual enthusiasm for kaiju eiga, Wilbur invited Tiffany out for a drink. Six months later, the two fans were married. Tiffany insists that, when she told Thorley this real-life fairy tale, he understood every word.

Eric Yamashita, as we all know, indeed managed to turn Gorgantis into a symbol for nuclear weapons abolition. While humankind has not yet taken the message to heart, Eric swears that he will never abandon the struggle. He really believes that one day our species will wake up and say, "Good God, what are we doing?"

We hope Eric and Tiffany are right when they insist that Thorley spent his nursing home sojourn in happy, if comatose, contemplation of his halcyon days. Until the very end, they claim, his brain was flooded with golden memories of tramping around graveyards, crypts, dungeons, and laboratories with the aim of giving pleasurable frissons to moviegoers, an ambition in which he was, as we all know, wholly successful. Visit the actor's modest marble tombstone, and you will find many tokens of esteem perched among the flowers: Corpuscula action figures, Kha-Ton-Ra rings, plush Gorgantis toys, even the robot from Flesh of Iron.

The appended notes are short and sweet. The one we transcribed on our last trip to Forest Lawn was typical, scrawled on a piece of shirt cardboard and secured beneath a pot of geraniums. Raindrops had blurred the ink, and the cardboard was badly warped, but we could still read every word.

Good-bye, dear Syms,

You were the best,
especially as Corpuscula,
and also the King of the Lizards.
We're sorry we never met you.

With gratitude,
Rose and Luís Rodriguez,
Your fans for life.